Ethan's
War

Ethan's War

Mike Harvey

Published by Mike Harvey, 2023.

This is a work of fiction. Similarities to real people, places, or events are entirely coincidental.

ETHAN'S WAR

First edition. March 27, 2023.

ISBN: 979-8224250516

Written by Mike Harvey.

Chapter One

The worst part of my day lies between the moment I wake up and the moment I open my eyes. I call it the storm before the storm. Sometimes, it is a long and lingering event, other times it is a panic-fueled rapid progression. This morning, it was a prolonged self-inflicted punishment. I could tell that I was laying on cool stone by the ache in my back and I began the mental investigation into where I might be and what could have caused me to end up here.

The first clue was the pounding, throbbing pain in the back of my head. I had imbibed pretty intensely in the wine; that was apparent. An all-too-frequent assumption these days. I remember the start of my day yesterday. I tended to the goats at my farm and then met Tabor early in the afternoon to start drinking. My stomach turned at the thought of my wine intake. I desperately tried to breathe slowly to push the nausea back down. I did not want to begin this day by vomiting in a mysterious location.

I was still not ready to open my eyes yet so I continued to think. After several rounds of sweet refreshments, I went to visit Padma. By this time, my memory had been reduced to short, random, and often confusing flashes. We continued to drink and that was when things spiraled out of control. I began to hope that it was still dark out so that when I opened my eyes, the sun would not exacerbate the pounding in my brain. Also, it would provide a cover for the shame that was ever-present these days.

I slowly opened my eyes and noticed that Padma was beside me. At least wherever I was, she was here with me. She looked beautiful in her slumber. She wore a white dress that barely covered her body in the rising sun, she was a vision to behold. She had long brown hair that descended far beyond her shoulders and she lay in a blissful sleep that seemed far too peaceful for the memories that I had just tried to navigate.

Her lips were still painted red. Was it cosmetic or from the wine? I loved those lips and longed to kiss them again like I had the night before. She had her right arm under her head as a pillow and a soft, mesmerizing, audible breathing emanated from her mouth. I knew from experience that her closed eyes were a deep, exotic blue and were very easy to get lost in. If I loved anything, it was her. Of course, I doubted my ability to truly love anyone or anything. I hated this daily routine but was helpless to break the cycle. Even now, I was planning where to get my next drink to ease the pain that reverberated throughout my entire body.

Next, I lowered my eyes to inspect my state of affairs. I had my white linen shirt on and noticed that I was only wearing my hagor, underwear, to cover my lower half. I saw one of my wooden sandals but from this perspective, the location of the other one was a mystery. Shame trickled through me all over again. I sat up and reignited waves of pain from my head down to my back. I looked around the dark room. Rays of sunlight had started streaming into the room and silhouettes of objects began to clarify. We had ended up at the altar of Ba'al again.

About six other bodies were laying in various states of undress all around the room and I was relieved to find them all still asleep. I didn't recognize anyone, so Tabor must have embarked on a separate journey apart from me. I stared at the statue of Ba'al and wished to feel something. I did not necessarily believe that the Canaanite deity was real but also knew better than to assume that he wasn't. If he was real, why was I experiencing this doomed feeling deep inside? After all, Padma was an altar "worker" and provided the services I remember indulging in last night. This was a sacred act and should make the gods happy. This thought provided no relief.

Padma stirred a bit and reached her hand over to touch mine. I extended my hand and held it briefly. I looked around and found my other garments and pulled them on, hoping for an undetected exit. I slipped my one wooden sandal on, found my other one, and put that on as well. Now, it was time to attempt to stand. Rambunctious nights like last night should not have these painful repercussions the next morning when you are in your early twenties so I must have drank more than normal. I stood as quietly as I could and began to walk to the door.

I knew that Padma would be upset with me for leaving without saying goodbye but I was humiliated and desperately wanted out of this setting as quickly as possible. I would later tell her that I was late for my duties at home and had to return before sunrise. She would still be hurt but would inevitably forgive me. She was usually paid for what she did for me last night, but our relationship was much deeper than she experienced with other worshippers. At least, that's what she told me and I tended to believe her.

I walked out the door and the city of Rimmon extended before me. Dirty, single-floor stone houses lined the dirt road and showed little to no signs of life at this early hour. Shadows may have hidden onlookers to witness my escape but they were discreet enough to not say anything if they did. I walked away from the temple towards my farm, starting to feel my blood flow return but I was still left uncertain about how productive I would be today. Checking the stone retaining walls to make sure the grapes received enough water was easy enough but cleaning out the irrigation ditches throughout the wheat fields could be grueling. Maybe I would just tend the goats and take a nap in the field. That sounded too tempting to pass up.

By the time I got home, the sun was beating down and it was already extremely hot. I had begun to sweat out all of the poison I had ingested the day before and would have done anything for some water to try and replenish my strength. I quietly opened the door, genuinely unsure whether my father would be sleeping or not. That question was answered immediately when I entered our tiny home. He lay underneath the single wooden table we owned with his wineskin in hand. I gently removed it and set it on the table as he began to stir.

He was going through his version of what I had already experienced at the altar. He sat up, nearly bumping his head on the table. As his eyes met mine, he looked embarrassed and turned away.

"Good morning, father. I was just about to eat something, get some water and start on the chores. How are you today?" I tried to greet him as gently as I could since I was in no position to judge. At least he indulged in his sin in the privacy of his own home. My mother had died several years before, during the night of the smoke, and it left him without anyone to regulate his behavior. It was extremely hard on both of us, but he simply seemed to give up.

"I am well, thank you." his voice cracked. He was obviously thankful that I did not address the situation before me. "I was going to run into town today and pick up some supplies. We do not have much but do you need anything?"

That was an understatement. We were the definition of impoverished but he always found the resources to secure more wine. Since that was all I was going to need anyway, I just shook my head. I popped a few dates in my mouth and went to the well to quench my thirst. I looked out over our farm and admired what we had been able to build. It was a modest farm but the revenue we were able to generate was sporadic at best. There was a wooden shed that I had constructed the year prior where some of our tools were kept and I headed in that direction. There was still some wine that was hidden there that had evaded my father's purview thus far. I would only drink a little to ease the shaking that was plaguing me. I would try to squeeze in a little work before once again going to Tabor's house to see where his night took him.

I ventured into the fields where the goats were and sat down amongst them. Guilt found me there as well. I had no direction. I had no moral compass that was driving me. I was a grown man amongst a proud people and felt completely unfit to call them my brethren. The Zebulun tribe of Israel was where I called home but I could not possibly feel more like a foreigner. Just southwest of the Sea of Galilee was considered sacred ground by my ancestors but they treated me like nothing more than a tawdry brothel attendee.

I wish that I felt some kindred connection to this land or its inhabitants. I wished I blindly believed in this Yahweh as others did, but there was an unholy absence of any conviction within me. The cycle needed to be broken but I saw no method of achieving this. The urge to cry washed over me but I was able to push it away by once again thinking of Padma. The thought of her always calmed me and for a second, I regretted departing from her without words this morning. She would undoubtedly be awake by now and probably feeling as though she was nothing more than a worthless temple prostitute that was simply used and discarded.

The only solution that I could come up with was to drink more wine to numb the nagging inferiority that was blinding me. As I did so, a little ambition began to take hold. I checked the retaining walls and noticed some blockages in the irrigation ditch. I half-heartedly used the hoe to remove them as best I could and vowed to come back later to do a more efficient job. For now, it was time to see Tabor. He would have more wine.

* * * * *

I surprised myself with the volume of work I was able to accomplish and the sun had already begun its decline when I set off for Tabor's. I was feeling better and told myself to take it easy today so that the chain of last night's calamity would not repeat itself.

When I reached Tabor's house, he had already started drinking as well. He had a flask in his hand when he saw me approaching.

"Ethan! The grand farmer of Rimmon. It is good to see you again, my friend. Would you like a drink?" Tabor greeted me cheerfully.

"I believe you already know the answer to that," I responded, trying not to sound as desperate as I felt. There was no more wine in my stash and my father would not be home from his trip into town until much later in the day. He handed me a wineskin that had been wrapped around his waist and I began to drink it much faster than I had originally intended to.

"How is the lovely Padma faring these days?" Tabor said with a mischievous grin spread across his face.

"Well, she was in good spirits last night..."

"I'm sure she was." Tabor interrupted.

"But..." I said with exaggerated disdain, "I left before she woke up this morning."

"She loves it when you do that," Tabor said, shaking his head. "How are you going to make it up to her?"

"I haven't thought that far ahead. I am just going to explain that I had to leave early to get my work done. She should understand." I muttered, not believing one single word that came out of my mouth.

"Yes. From what I have learned of women over my many years, they have always proven to be understanding. They also love when you leave mysteriously without saying goodbye after a night of passionate intimacy"

I cringed. "We are the same age and I would argue that you have learned very little about women. I have many stories in my arsenal to prove that point." Tabor was almost as reliable as Padma when it came to improving my spirits.

"I have learned enough to know that those who worship Ba'al tend to be more fun than those who worship Yahweh, that's for sure. I have a couple of stories from last night to prove my point as well if you would like to hear them."

"I most certainly do not, thank you. I shudder at the mere thought of your experiences much less hearing them told in the form of your prose. How do you manage to wake up feeling so alive and filled with purpose the next day? I felt inches from death this morning." I responded while finishing my drink.

"You just happened to be cursed with a conscience. I was born devoid of any such affliction." Tabor said, still smiling broadly. I was jealous of his confidence and with the ease that he carried himself. He never seemed to be riddled with doubt like I was.

"Does Ba'al not have such moral standards that you must adhere to?"

"How would I know?" Tabor said with a laugh.

"Do you not worship at the altar of Ba'al? Do you lack all knowledge of his ways?" I said incredulously.

"I never said I believed in him, I just like to *worship* him. There is a huge difference, my friend. To believe in something requires investment. You must study the writings and learn of his ways. I have no time for such trivial exercises. I am perfectly content with my current trajectory to be swayed by unseen forces I have no control over."

"Therein lies the difference between us. I do wish to invest. I just don't have the first clue as to where to devote my efforts." I said as I looked at the ground in frustration.

Tabor wrapped his arm around me to comfort me, "Don't be so hard on yourself, Ethan. That is why the gods made wine! I can think of no better investment than that."

That was exactly what I was afraid of.

Chapter Two

We sat down at a table in the wine shop as dusk set in. I had paced myself better today but still felt the effects of what I had drank so far. In what was turning out to be one of the longest days I could remember, I looked around the shop as we waited to order a drink and noticed that a few of the same people were here from yesterday. Had they even left? I ran my fingers through my hair and took a deep breath, trying to remember to pace myself.

As our drinks were placed in front of us, I quickly took a deep draw from the rim of the cup. I looked up and a stunning woman about five foot six was walking up behind Tabor. She had long, black hair that ran wild all the way to the small of her back. She had large, round brown eyes and dark makeup that accentuated her perfect features. She gently placed her hand on the back of Tabor's neck and started to rub. Without looking up, he smiled that smile he always flashed and leaned into the massage.

"I recognize those fingertips anywhere." He said as he closed his eyes.

"You better." The woman said as she walked around him and sat between us in one of the two empty chairs at our table. "Where have you been lately?" she asked in a sultry voice. She wore the same garb that Padma wore and I recognized her from the altar which started my day. I knew her name was Dabria and had seen her around but was much too intimidated to ever pay her any special attention.

"I've been recuperating from our last encounter. It takes a man a long time to recover from your attention. You should be flattered." Tabor responded without missing a beat. I don't know how he did it. He seemed so at ease with everyone, man or woman, that he encountered. It had taken all the nerve that I could muster to simply talk to Padma for the first time and she was paid to be with men professionally.

"I would be flattered if I thought there was a sliver of truth somewhere in that statement." Dabria countered while stealing a drink of Tabor's wine.

"Why would I lie to my favorite girl?" He leaned over to try and give her a kiss but she turned him away. There was no real malice in the gesture, it was just a game the two of them played.

"I can think of a few reasons. Anyway, Padma is quite upset with you, young man." Dabria said as she turned her gaze to me. I felt my heart begin to race. I couldn't tell if it was because this dazzling creature had acknowledged me or it was the mention of Padma.

"I...I had to work early this morning." I stammered, the excuse sounding pathetic and empty.

"Women don't usually tend to appreciate that line. I would come up with something else before you see her again." She squinted her eyes and seemed to analyze me more carefully. I immediately felt uncomfortable and turned my attention back to my cup of wine.

Tabor wrapped his arm around her and tried to kiss her neck but she only intensified her gaze on my face. "I can see what she sees in you. There is something in your eyes." She allowed Tabor his advances but her focus on me was unsettling.

"She is a special woman." was all I could think to say.

She held her gaze a moment later and then leaned back into Tabor's arm and put her left hand under the table into his leg. It was a brazen display of affection that was probably all too common in this type of establishment. "Anyway, she expects to see you tonight so you better come up with something. I would bring an offering to make it more *official* tonight. You wouldn't want the temple priests thinking she is giving away her services for free now would you?"

I blushed at her forward nature and took another drink. I had to be careful. My head was beginning to swim in the wine and I could feel I was on the brink of another tornadic night. Dabria had expedited my drinking with her presence and I had to fight the urge to finish off my drink.

There was an awkward, prolonged silence while Dabria and Tabor engaged in their affections and finally, she said, "I want to show you something out back." With that, the two disappeared out the door and I was thankfully left alone to regroup. Just then, an enormous man emerged from the burgeoning crowd and sat down in the opposite chair that Dabria had just occupied.

"Unfortunately, I knew I could find you here. How are you, old friend?" The man pushed the Tabor's wine further away from him like it was some sort of toxin.

I collected myself for fear of slurring my words and said, "I'm good, Amos. How are you?" The man looked at me, studying me to make sure I was not drunk and would remember this encounter at a later time. Amos was one of my oldest friends, therefore he knew how hard I could drink and the ramifications that stemmed from this cycle. He was gigantic in stature. He stood at least six foot five feet tall and had curly brown hair down to his shoulders. He had a sharp nose and astute eyes that seemed to take everything in. He had never had a sip of wine and took pride in his righteous behavior. Despite this, I adored the man.

"I'm well thank you. I just came by to give you a little warning."

I was not in the mood to hear about how much I drink and I subtly rolled my eyes at his attempt to sober me up. "What should I be aware of?" I asked, not wanting to hear his response.

"I just got back from Megiddo."

"How is old Deborah?" I asked. He was always reminding me that he was an important figure in the house of the great Jewish judge. Normally, this pretentious sort of behavior would irritate me, but Amos received a pass in my book for some reason.

"She is on the move. She is getting ready to fight and word has it they are going to Hazor to take the land back. This would be a big opportunity for someone who is looking for something honorable to achieve in this life."

That was an obvious dig. Had I told him about my most recent crisis of conscience? I don't remember having this conversation with him but that would not be unusual. I don't remember a lot of conversations I have. Anyway, I haven't seen Amos in quite a few months so had I really been droning on about my lack of direction for that long?

"That is big news. I am hardly a soldier like you though. If I took up arms against a well-trained Canaanite army, I would surely be cut in half within seconds of the start of any aggression. Do you forget I spend my day's herding goats and growing a moderate amount of wheat and grapes? That has hardly prepared me for swinging a sword."

"That is not what I am warning you about. Aggression in one region inevitably leads to nervous leaders in every region. The Midianites have been increasing their raids into the Jezreel Valley as of late as well. I just thought you should be alert and ready for any bands that might take a little too kindly to your modest farm. I know your father..."

Is a hopeless drunk? Unable to defend our land? We both knew how that sentence was going to end but he graciously passed on the opportunity to point out the obvious.

"I just want you to be safe. You are my oldest friend and I don't want you to fall prey to those heathens from the east. Anyway, There is another man you will no doubtedly hear about in the near future. They call him Jerubbaal. He is openly rebelling and destroying altars of Ba'al and upsetting the masses with his disdain for local gods."

I immediately returned my thoughts to Padma and feared for her safety. She was the only thing good in my life and if something should happen to her, I would be even more lost.

"What about you? Where are you going off to?" I asked, desperately trying to change the subject away from anything related to Padma.

"I'll be here for a while but I am heading up to join Deborah again. That is where the action is going to be. The Canaanites and Midianites have been wreaking havoc on all of us and this obsession with Ba'al has led to many living in absolute poverty."

"Did the word Ba'al just come out of your mouth?" Tabor bellowed as he reentered the shop and retained his seat.

Amos rolled his eyes and leaned back. "Only to complain about the pagans who worship him. I should have known you would be here." Amos' disgust with Tabor was palpable and when he picked up his wine and finished it in one large gulp dramatically, Amos rolled his eyes again.

"This subject has come up quite often the past couple of days. Shouldn't you be espousing the one and only Yahweh as the most great and powerful?" I hated how Tabor baited Amos but their entire relationship was built on this type of back and forth.

"He is and you would be wise to stay away from those pagan temples you like to frequent. Worshiping that false deity in private may be safer for you in the long run." Amos said, surprisingly offering a bit of concern for my friend.

"You think that is what I'm doing? I couldn't possibly care less about Ba'al. I'm just there because the people are more fun to be around than you pious Jews. They could worship a candlestick for all I care, but do go on about your mighty Yahweh. If he is so powerful, why would he bother to give one thought about so-called *false deities*?"

"I don't have the time nor the inclination to explain to you such things. My words would fall on deaf ears so I'll save them for people who matter."

"Like our friend Ethan, here?" Tabor said as he put his hand on my shoulder. He was in an even better mood now that he had been with Dabria, who hadn't bothered to even come back into the wine shop.

"Leave me out of your bickering." I said half-heartedly.

"No. You, my friend, are a lost soul. You need inspiration. Has Amos told you all about the one, all-powerful Yahweh?"

"I've done my pondering on the matter. I just don't feel his presence like Amos does and that is fine. We don't have to dwell on it." I didn't like discussing this in front of Amos. He was so passionate about serving his Lord and I was passionate about...wine.

Amos folded his arms and stared at Tabor, "As a matter of fact, we have had many discussions on that topic. I fear that your influence undoes everything I try to accomplish."

Tabor chuckled, "I'm not sure you know what *all-powerful* means then."

Amos stood up abruptly, "That's it. I've hit my limit with this one." Amos turned from Tabor and looked at me. "Be ready tomorrow. I'm taking you hunting. I need a little peace and quiet before I leave. I'll be there in the morning so take it easy tonight." With that, Amos turned to leave, obviously judging each and every person he passed on the way out.

"What a lovely fellow. I actually do have a fondness for him despite the fact he despises me." Tabor said as he signaled for two more drinks. I started to tell him not to, but I needed another one after that conversation. "How exciting for you, though. A hunting trip early in the morning. That should be a lot of fun!"

"Your wit is unmatched, Tabor. I like hanging out with Amos. I know he is a little dry, but he has a good heart. He's done more with his life than I have." I relented while taking a drink from my newly filled cup.

"I wouldn't say that. Padma is quite an achievement. Speaking of which, how about we finish these cups and go do a little *offering* at the altar?"

I thought for a few long seconds, trying to find bravery in my words. "I don't know if I want to go back there anymore. For the past seven years, we have all lived in fear of raiders and armies from the East. From what Amos just told me, there is a man south of here now destroying pagan idols and altars. It could be dangerous on two fronts now."

"Life is danger. Padma is the reward. Drink a little more courage and we'll go settle things so that you aren't in trouble anymore."

I am weak. I finished my drink and the second the last drop went down my throat, I knew that I had gone too far. I had reached the point in the evening where decision-making was a thing of the past. I was simply along for Tabor's ride. I knew that tomorrow morning was going to be an exercise in misery but I had already fully committed to debauchery and there was no more turning back.

Chapter Three

The sun's attempts to wake me up were cruel in nature. The storm before the storm. I lay on my mattress and was thankful that the night before had brought me here. The daily routine of trying to piece together the night before was again a challenge. I remembered seeing Padma and offering some of the grapes that we had grown at the altar of Ba'al. I remember lying in her arms and earning her forgiveness. That was when the memories came to a screeching halt.

I must have walked home and that was a good sign. I heard my father snoring on the other side of the room and determined that it was safe to open my eyes. The sun brought harsh judgment on my condition and I reached to my left to grab the wineskin from the night before. Thankfully I had left some for the morning. The night version of myself was looking out for the morning me!

I took a healthy swig and forced myself up on my elbows. The one-room hovel was in its usual disarray but there likely would be no time to clean up before Amos arrived. Unfortunately, he was a man of his word and he would be here at any minute. I stretched and made it to my feet. I made my way to the well outside and splashed some water on my face just in time to hear my friend approach.

"Good morning, Ethan. I see that you survived the night."

Barely.

"I was eager to see you, friend. I came home almost immediately and began preparing for our trip." I had no idea where this compulsion to lie came from, but it was there nonetheless.

"I'm sure you did. I figured we would head east toward the sea of Galilee and see what enters our path. Are you ready?" Amos said, tying his sling closer to his waist. An axe and a long hunter's knife were tied to the other side of his waist.

"Just let me get a couple of things and check on my father and we'll be on our way." I said, heading back into the house. I was thankful when Amos didn't follow me. I was embarrassed by the condition of our home and didn't want him to see my father, drunk on the floor.

"Father, I am heading out with Amos on a little hunting trip. Do you need anything before I go?" I shook him as I gently tried to wake him up. It took quite a bit of jostling but he eventually stirred from his drunken slumber.

"What? Oh, no. I'm ok. Good luck. We are running low on food so may your trip be productive and fruitful." He said as he jolted awake. I got my hunting knife and bow and by the time I walked out the door, my father was asleep again. Depending on how long my trip took, I assumed he would be in the same position when I returned. I glanced at the wineskin that lay beside him and picked it up. It was full and I was just a bit ashamed when I took it and tied it beneath my loincloth. It couldn't hurt to have a spare nip while out in the woods.

"My father is getting ready for the day, but he sends his greetings." I said to Amos as I emerged from the house. We both knew I was lying, but Amos nodded in agreement anyway.

"This farm has quite a bit of potential. Do you like it here?" Amos said as we began to walk east toward the forest.

I looked down at my feet and thought for a moment. "It is as good a spot as any to be in, I guess." That was honest enough. I truly did not mind the farming life, but times had been hard as of late. The tribes of Israel had been brutally hit by invaders from the east, even if none had physically tampered with my own stock.

"I do not mean to disparage your life's work, I truly don't, but have you given any thought to taking up arms to defend our land?" Amos said while staring at me intently. I looked over at him. He was so muscular as if chiseled from marble. Of course, he was willing to fight. Look at him. He could surely handle any weapon that was put in his hands.

"We are not all as physically gifted as you are, my friend. I would only inspire confidence in the enemy if I stood opposite them on the battlefield. I do not think a soldier's life is for me."

"This is not a gift." Amos said with a smirk while he flexed his biceps. "This is discipline and hard work. Soldiers come in all shapes and sizes, by the way. Not everyone who serves under the judge looks like me. I have seen you shoot your bow and you are handy with tools. You could offer your services in a myriad of ways."

"It is definitely something I will pray about." Another lie slipped easily from my tongue.

"And who will those prayers be directed to?" Amos asked. It seemed like an innocuous question but I knew enough to suspect it was loaded.

I looked straight ahead and something came over me. Surprising myself, I decided to try a little honesty in my response. "I'll be honest with you, Amos. I'm not sure I even know how to pray. I know the answer you're looking for is Yahweh, but I don't even know the words to speak."

Amos nodded in startling empathy. "Yahweh is our heavenly father. You can talk to him just like that. You have talked to your own father, have you not?"

I chuckled a bit, "I have, but no deity wants to hear what I say to him."

"Try asking him for directions. Ask him what your purpose is and what you should do to best honor and serve him. He has a way of revealing things to us."

"If He is so powerful and all-knowing, why do I not hear him clearly? Why has Israel been overrun by these pagans and heathens that you speak of? Every Israelite I know lives in abject poverty. I thought we were His chosen people. I have never felt *chosen* for anything other than a life of misery and filled with mindless toiling."

Amos seemed to ponder this for a moment and then offered, "We have turned our backs on him. There are more altars of Ba'al than to Him…"

"I do not worship nor believe in Ba'al. I hope you know that." I interrupted, knowing that was where this conversation was eventually going to end up.

"I'm not saying that. I would never claim to know another man's heart, but do your actions reflect that? As I said, I am not judging, that is Yahweh's job, but what you do is just as important as what you believe."

"I think my actions reflect my heart perfectly. It is undecided, unsure and uncertain. It seems like all I can think about now is this woman. She is not a believer in Yahweh, though, and that presents a challenge for any Jew."

"But she does believe in Ba'al?" Amos asked, genuinely curious.

"To be honest, I don't think she does. It is simply a role to her that has been passed to her by her ancestors. I think she is more like me in the fact that she simply doesn't know what she believes in." This conversation had come up before with Padma. She hated her status in life but like me, had no idea how to change it. It seems like we lived in a time where someone was born into their life's work, devoid of any real choice.

"The only advice I can offer you on such matters is to start surrounding yourself with people who make you better, who inspire you to be more."

"I assume you don't think Tabor is that person?" I asked, already knowing the answer.

"He most definitely is not. I hate to say it, but I believe he does not have a long life in his future. He lives fast and reckless and brings you along for every moment of it."

"He makes me laugh."

"There is more to life than merriment. The beginning of belief is contemplation. How much of your time is spent pondering the existence of our Lord?" Amos said, sounding a little more judgmental with each retort.

"It seems like a lot lately. It has come up quite often in conversation as of late."

"But do you meditate on it? Do you spend time in solitude, truly questioning things." Amos said, his gaze intensifying as we walked.

"I begin to, but my mind can't grasp the immensity of it all. I am riddled with doubt and do not wish to appear foolish, placing my beliefs in something that may not be real."

"That is your downfall, Ethan. Ever since I have known you when we were children playing in the dirty streets of Rimmon, you have only ever wanted everyone you meet to like you. It is a worldly desire to so desperately seek the approval of everyone you encounter."

That was true. For as long as I remember, all I wanted was to be liked. I don't know if it stemmed from my low standing in society, but I truly despise confrontation and simply want to be known as agreeable. This was probably how I ended up in the cycle I was currently trapped in.

Just then, we heard a stir up ahead of us coming from a grove of olive trees. We both stopped immediately and our hands went to our weapons. Amos squinted his eyes and we dared not move a muscle. A camel emerged from behind a trunk that it was apparently tied to. He gently stepped forward toward the out-of-place creature.

Amos drew his axe and placed his other hand on the nose of the camel as we both looked around. Suddenly, a man dressed in nomadic garb stepped from some bushes that had kept him concealed. His face displayed his shock at seeing two strangers so close by. How he had not heard our conversation upon approach, I'll never know but we had in fact, taken him completely by surprise.

The man recovered and drew his sword quickly. I could tell by the look in his eyes that he had every intention of using it as he slowly stepped forward. To my surprise, Amos returned his axe to his waist and stepped forward to meet him. Swiftly, Amos clenched his fist and used it to land a square punch to the man's nose. Blood squirted from the man's face and he stumbled backward just a bit. Before he could draw his sword back, Amos landed another punch to the man's left cheek.

The second punch sent the man to his back and Amos was atop him almost instantly. During this altercation, I had not moved a muscle. Amos raised his fist and promptly hit him in the face several more times. He placed his enormous hands on either side of the nomad's face and violently twisted the man's neck until he lay awkward and motionless on the ground. Within seconds, Amos had killed the stranger.

He sat on top of the man for a moment, breathing heavily. Moments later, we heard footsteps moving rapidly away from us, indicating that there were more men in hiding that wanted to avoid us, or more specifically, Amos.

Amos stood and then I saw the blood streaked across his white linen outerwear. He had a look in his eyes that could only be described as bloodlust and I wondered how he reconciled what he had just done with his concept of Yahweh. I walked over to him and put my hand on his shoulder to gauge how he was feeling. He looked up at me and smiled just a bit. That was not what I was expecting.

"There were at least two other Midianites over there. Did you hear that?" He said through clenched teeth.

"I did. I am glad they chose to run." I said, taking a deep breath of relief.

"I am not." He said the words so convincingly that it left no doubt in my mind that they would have suffered the same fate as the man who lay behind us.

"I do have a question for you, though." I asked as I turned my attention to the camel that apparently belonged to us now. "When he drew his sword, you sheathed your axe. What is the purpose of carrying weapons if you are just going to murder someone with your bare hands?"

"Let me ask you something. If you want to prove to someone that you are as powerful as you are, do you use all the weapons in your arsenal? No, you use as little as possible so that the man knows how strong you truly are. If I had killed him with an axe, the other Midianites could have just assumed I got in a lucky strike. Using my hands, I showed them that I was no one to be meddled with."

"I see your point. You knew there were other Midianites close by?" I asked. I had not heard nor seen them until after the brief entanglement.

He smiled broadly, "No."

Chapter 4

When I returned home later that day, I found my father out in the fields, staring off into the distance. This was an odd spectacle to behold since he had no drink in hand. I walked up to him, assuming he heard my approach. When I greeted him, he was startled back to reality.

"Did you bring home any food?" He asked, trying to regain his composure.

"Apparently, it was not that kind of hunting trip." I said, worried that something was wrong with him. His hands were shaking and his eyes looked tired. "What are you doing out here father?"

"Just checking on the goats. I might head into town in a little bit."

"I will see you later then." I said as I walked to the well to get a drink of water. As soon as my father left, I took the wineskin I had stowed away and took a long drink from it. I felt sorry for my father. He had lost the love of his life and stayed in an inebriated state at any given moment of the day. If he had any strong beliefs regarding Yahweh or even Ba'al, he had never shared them with me. I used to be angry at the lack of parental involvement, but now that I had picked up his vice, I understood him and even began to empathize with him.

The prospect of staying home with nothing to do did not interest me and I doubted I had the constitution for another round of drinking with Tabor, so I headed to the altar to try and lure Padma away. It was always a precarious venture to walk into the temple unannounced for I did not want to witness Padma with another worshiper, but that was exactly what happened. I knew that others meant nothing to her, but it was still a sight that I did not wish to see.

To make matters worse, the man who had presented offerings was treating her more violently than he should have. Fury rose into my throat and I stepped forward. Her eyes met mine and a strange mix of emotions swirled within them. She looked ashamed and terrified that I would intervene. By stopping his *worship* I would dishonor Ba'al and more importantly, Padma. She subtly waved me back outside. Everything inside of me wanted to rip the man off of her and handle him as Amos did with the Midianite but I fought the urge and turned back around. I found a bench outside the temple and tried to restore my breathing back to normal.

I put my head in my hands and fought back tears of anger...or sadness. I couldn't tell but I was much too tired to contemplate the origin. Even at my most optimistic, I could not see a path for Padma and me to make a life for ourselves. I often lay awake at night, when not obliterated, and tried to plan our future but it was not to be. With the rush of emotions I was feeling, I was pretty sure this was the closest that I had come to determine that we should not be together anymore. I was about to get up and walk away when Daria put her hand on my shoulder.

"It means nothing to her. You know that right?"

I looked intently into Daria's eyes and nodded. She was entirely entrancing. If I had no feelings for Padma, I would say she was the most beautiful woman I had ever seen. Every movement of her body was an enchanted seduction.

"It's still difficult to witness." I finally stated as I broke eye contact with her.

"You are the one that she wants a life with. You have to know that."

"And how exactly would that work? Is she going to walk away from the temple and come help out on the farm?" My sarcasm was more vitriolic than I had intended but it was borne of pain.

"She is one of my best friends, and I would hate to see her leave, but maybe you could start over somewhere else. Create a life out of thin air." I looked back at Daria and she stared ahead as if picturing the scene.

"You know as well as I do that picking up and moving to a new city would make us outsiders. Foreigners do not fare very well in strange cities. I have considered it a thousand times, but I do not think it is a viable option."

She put her hand back on my shoulder and stood up to leave. I don't know if it was in my head, but she left her hand to linger longer than seemed normal. Was she offering an invitation? Her fingers slid off my shoulders as she made her way back into the temple. It was at that moment that Padma exited. It was too late. I couldn't leave now. I dropped my head and stared at the ground as she made her way to me.

"I'm so sorry you had to see that." She said as she put her hand on my leg. I wanted to knock her hand away, but that would have destroyed her. I could hear tears in her voice as she offered her apologies. I tried to be a bigger man and think of something to say.

"Can we go somewhere else? I do not wish to be here any longer than I have to."

"Of course. Let me clean up and we can go wherever you like."

My stomach turned at the thought of her having to *clean up* but I just nodded. I quickly tried to think of where we could go but my mind kept returning to the wine shop. I needed a drink but did not want to run into Tabor tonight. By the time Padma returned, I had formulated a plan in my head.

"Let's have a picnic somewhere far away from anyone else in the world. I would like to be alone with you." Her smile lit up her face. The sun struck her eyes and they sparkled with pure unadulterated joy.

"I would absolutely love that!"

"First, I need you to do me a small favor. I will run home and prepare some food if you could stop by the wine shop and purchase some, that would be great. Tell the owner it is for me. I have an account there. I will meet you at the foot of the rock, in the pomegranate grove."

"That sounds wonderful. I will meet you there as soon as I can." She kissed me on the cheek as I tried not to remember what I had witnessed only moments before. I went home and was thankful that my father had left. I did not want to answer any questions he may have. I prepared a dinner of cooked chevon and grapes. I finished off the wine that I had secured for my trip with Amos, which now seemed a lifetime ago.

My entire trip to the pomegranate grove was filled with an internal lecture that I gave to myself to forgive her and not ruminate on what had happened at the temple. I just kept repeating that it was not her fault and it did not matter. When I reached a spot that would all but guarantee our solitude, I laid out a cloth blanket and started to set the food out.

She emerged from the trees, a stunning vision of beauty. She had donned a blue dress that was elegant and form-fitting. Her long, curly brown hair seemed to bounce as she giggled her way to me. She sat on the blanket and leaned over to greet me with a long, tender kiss.

"This is just what I needed. Thank you so much."

I couldn't help but smile back and said, "You are more than welcome. This is the best that I could do with what I had." I said modestly. I started to ask how her day had been but caught myself. Navigating through a normal conversation with her would be a challenge, so I simply said, "You look beautiful." as the sun set behind her.

She smiled as she poured the wine and I tried not to appear too eager in taking my first drink. My second and third drinks quickly followed as I tried to think of what to talk about. Thankfully, she initiated.

"What did you do today?"

I took a deep breath and shook my head. "I had quite an interesting day. I took a trip with my friend Amos. We encountered some Midianites that were not from around here." I debated going any further since it had suddenly occurred to me that I knew nothing of her background. I only assumed that she was not a Jew.

"Many have attended the temple lately. I hear they have wreaked havoc on many of the farms and fields as of late."

The statement indicated that she held no particular affection for them, or at the very least, she was not one of them so I continued.

"Well, the one that we encountered will not ever visit the temple."

"What happened to him?" She asked, almost matching her wine intake with mine.

I looked into her eyes, unsure how to phrase what I had seen. "My friend Amos is not an avid supporter of the Midianites as a whole, so he..." I didn't know how to finish the sentence, but she drew her own conclusion and looked downward in sadness.

"I hate violence. I don't much like the Midianites, either, but I don't like the idea of taking any life. This world is full of too much violence for my taste."

"I'm not prone to it as well, but a man has to take a stand when his livelihood is threatened. Israelites go without food and supplies while they simply steal and kill at their own leisure. It is not right."

"Do you believe that this land belongs to the Israelites?" It was a heavy question that she did not ask lightly. No malice was behind the words, I do not believe there was any within her, but it was still somewhat of a challenge.

"Well, my people believe that this land was promised to them by the Lord." I was curious to see how she would handle such an assertion.

She shook her head and responded with, "Most violence I witness originates with deities. I think a man would be better off not acknowledging any such notion."

"So you don't believe in the worship of Ba'al or Yahweh?"

"That is a deeply personal question." she gasped, shocked. I could point out what I had witnessed earlier as an even more personal practice but reminded myself to not shame her.

"I'm aware, but when you feel strongly about another person, it is important to get to know what motivates them, what they believe in. I do care for you. I care for you more than just about anyone I know. If I am too forward, it is only because I want to know everything about you." Apparently, the wine had taken effect, for I had never been so aggressive in detailing my affection for her.

She smiled, somewhat embarrassed, and responded by giving me another kiss. "I care for you as well, Ethan. I care for you more than anyone else on this earth. My parents gave me to the temple as an offering when I was a baby and I have never known my family. The times I see you are the only thing that brings me joy." She paused, searching for an answer. "I don't believe I have much use for any god, real or imagined. They have done nothing for me. The men who come to *worship* put on a good showing, but I know they just want to satisfy their own personal lust."

"I would say you are probably correct in that assumption. I would argue that there would probably be just as much if not more violence in the absence of any heavenly being. Violence is in man's nature."

"Not all men." She said as she smiled at me.

"No. Not all men. But I do sometimes find solace in the idea that Yahweh is a heavenly father that loves his people as his own children. My earthly father has not exactly been a shining example of paternal fortitude. I just find that I am too uncertain to throw my devotion towards something so grand and unseen."

"You are worried about looking foolish if you are wrong?" She asked innocently.

I squinted my eyes and thought about it. Is that what I was afraid of or was I just afraid to admit that I was one colossal disappointment to someone who apparently loves me so much?

"I don't know. I've thought about it a lot lately. Amos has said that there is a potential rebellion starting to form amidst the Jewish leaders and he has invited me to join the ranks."

Padma donned a worried expression and asked, "You aren't going to go, are you?"

"I had considered it. I find that I am not contributing to any greater good here. I run a small farm and have no impact on the world. What good do I bring to the world other than some goats and grapes." I shuddered as I heard the words spoken out loud. I sounded like a pouting toddler.

If I was not mistaken, Padma almost looked offended, "I just said that you were the only thing that brings me joy in this world. Are you saying that is not a worthy impact?"

"I'm not saying that at all."

"Are you saying you don't believe me?"

"That's not it." The conversation was spiraling out of control and I didn't know how to save it. "I said I had considered going, but it was because of you that I am not." I took a long drink of the wine in my hand, hoping that she would not be angry.

"I should hope not. To go and fight for a god that you may or may not believe in does not seem an effective way to extend one's life." Padma conceded.

"If I did decide to go, it would be because of my ancestors. Not because of Yahweh."

"How many of your ancestors do you know?" The question appeared to be made harshly and she knew it. She quickly tried to lessen the blow, "I didn't mean that the way it sounded. I just meant that I have never heard you talk about your family."

"It's fine. I have only met my father. My mother died long ago, during the night of the smoke, and apparently, my grandparents have chosen to disown my father."

"That is horrible. What happened on the night of the smoke?" Padma exclaimed.

"Well. My father has not exactly lived up to anyone's expectations. I love him, but he definitely...has his faults. You have never heard of the night of the smoke?"

"No. What happened?"

"When I was just a young boy, I would pester my father to take me to the caves above Rimmon. I used to love to sleep up there and get a good view of the surrounding lands. One night, I was choked awake by an acrid stench. Smoke filled the cave and I could barely breathe. I tried desperately to escape the cave but my father kept holding me back. He put his tunic over my nose and mouth and held me down. He didn't want me to see what was outside. We waited a couple of days and returned and my mother was gone. My father told me that she had died during the night of the smoke and that was it. He never went into further detail and I never pressed him on it."

"I'm so sorry." Padma said in a pitiful voice. She then tried to change the subject, seeing my discomfort. "Have you ever thought about starting a family?" Padma asked, eyes almost pleading.

"I have. You?"

Apparently, my answer was lacking because disappointment flooded her features. She looked away and finished her wine. "Who would want to start a family with a temple whore? You do know why your people have fallen into disfavor with Yahweh, don't you?"

I took her hand fiercely and stared into her eyes and said harshly, "Remember this moment. Remember everything about it because it will be the last time you *ever* use that word to describe yourself! To answer your question, no. I don't know why our God has forsaken us. Do you?"

Padma averted her gaze as if dreading the revelation she was about to speak life into. "Your people were supposed to massacre all of the Canaanites and people of the east. When you only conquered the army and began to live amongst us, it was an abomination against His will." A tear formed in her eyes and she leaned forward and kissed me. Those were the last words we spoke for a long time. We lay back on the blanket and for the longest time, I just held her. We didn't feel the need to talk about our pasts or our futures, the moment was enough. As I listened to her breathe, I wondered if there was any way that we could begin a family. I just didn't see how loving this tender, golden-hearted woman could ever anger a just God.

I was becoming too inebriated to contemplate such issues anymore and settled on one final thought. At least now I knew that I would not be joining Amos when he returned to the other rebellious Israelites. It was the first time that home actually gave me a warm feeling. Imagine how warm it would be with Padma's presence.

"I love you Padma." The words slipped out but were genuine and true.

She stirred a bit and looked up at me and gently kissed my lips.

"Then do so. With all of your heart. I have always felt that when you find love, you have to chase after it as if it were your last breath. I love you as well and will follow your lead. I will be by your side for as long as you will have me."

"It appears we will just have to forge our own path then." I finally said. She smiled up at me and kissed me again. I smiled to myself, if I wasn't careful, I was going to find purpose and direction once and for all.

Chapter 5

Sometimes, when mired in misery, one can lose track of the little moments that contribute. Coming home has always been just one in a myriad of daily moments that cause intense consternation. In addition to the mundane farmwork, never knowing the state of my father added a level of dread I had not been able to articulate. Now that I was experiencing hope for the first time, I was able to see unhealthy patterns where they hid in the darkness just days before.

This time was different. I was in love and I knew that someone loved me. I had not worked out the details just yet on how we would move forward, but at least forward was a direction. Adding to my sense of elation was the fact that I had not overindulged during my dinner with Padma. It seemed her presence had been enough for me this evening. Other evenings were designed for the sole purpose of satisfying the pleasures of the flesh, but tonight was different.

The sun was setting over the plains of Israel and the light that had so harshly judged me each morning, now seemed like it was making a peace offering of potential. I walked in our house and my father was sitting at the table with a drink in hand. This was not surprising but I felt that I was equipped to deal with it this evening.

He looked up and offered a half-smile. His eyes seemed to question whether I was going to ignore the wine or address it.

"Hello, father. How was your day?" I said, trying to put him at ease. He leaned back in his chair and took a deep breath.

"Oh, about the same as any other. I was able to do some chores and I think everything is done. How was your evening? I am surprised you are not out with Tabor."

"I need a break from Tabor." I said, pulling up a chair opposite him.

"Is everything ok between the two of you?" He asked, genuinely concerned.

"It's fine. I spent the evening with a nice, young lady." I said with a smile. Trying to drive the conversation to something positive for a change. With so many topics that we had to avoid, the rules of engagement with my father could be very tricky.

"How wonderful! What is her name?" I was shocked. He did not often show interest in my affairs and I wondered how brave I would be in revealing my newly minted plans.

"It was perfect. In fact, it was so perfect, I only slightly hesitate to say that I believe that I am in love with her. How do you feel about that? Her name is Padma." I did not expect an admonishment. He had given up on trying to steer me the right way years ago. I think he knew he would drown in the irony if he tried. I did half-expect apathy, though. Instead, his eyes lit up for the first time that I can remember. It was as if life had flooded back into his brittle, drunken body.

"That is wonderful to hear! I assume that she feels the same?" He questioned.

I smiled back at him, enjoying our rare back and forth, "Why do you assume that?"

"Who couldn't be enamored with you? You have turned into a fine young man. Any girl should be thankful to have you."

I opened my mouth, but nothing came out. I fought back tears from the rare compliment. "She claims to. I choose to take her at her word."

He nodded. Joy looked foreign to him, but I would cherish it nonetheless. "Is she Jewish?"

Here comes the hard part. If he had not buckled at the idea of his son being in love, this was where it could have all fallen apart. I looked down at the table and forced myself on, "She is unfortunately not."

He did not hesitate in response, "That is ok. We can make it work."

We? I was again taken aback by his declaration of optimism. "I'm glad to hear you say that. She is filled with love and kindness. There is not a malicious bone in her body and she will make you proud."

He smiled even bigger and a few moments of silence passed. "I'm sure she will. Let us take tomorrow off and I will clean up nicely. I would love to meet Padma."

His shoulders stiffened as he sat up a little straighter, obviously proud that he remembered her name. Tomorrow might be a different story but I will take the victory at hand rather than worry about the future's happenings.

"That sounds glorious. I will call on her in the morning and see when it would be good for her."

He stood up, relatively sure on his feet. He walked to the door and said, "We can make this work." He repeated, almost to himself. "We can build another structure in the clearing by the grape fields so you can have some privacy but we would still be close. That could work."

I sat back and just watched hope wash over him. In his mind, he really did believe that this was going to happen. I did as well, I was just surprised to see the enthusiasm in his demeanor for a change. It suited him well.

* * * * *

I lay in bed, trying to fight back the fears that crowded my thoughts. What if my father did not remember the conversation we had the day before? What if he had changed his mind? What if her ancestry suddenly became an issue for him? What if, in his newfound happiness, he justified drinking too much and embarrassed all parties involved? Mind you, none of these ponderings were helpful in nature, but they still plagued me.

I could not worry about such things. I got up and went out to the well. I passed my father, still sleeping on the floor. He had stayed up much later than me so I was not sure how much he had had to drink. I splashed water on my face and looked skyward.

"Yahweh. If you are real, please bless this union. Amos told me to talk to you like a father. I don't have a good example of one here on earth, so this is all I can offer. If I can have just this, I would be happy for the rest of my life. If you are a loving God, you should nurture it wherever it can be found in this hopeless, desolate land."

I finished freshening up and went to my shed. I found the wineskin that I had hidden from my father. I was so proud that I had not overindulged last night. Did I really need a drink now? Things were moving fast and I needed a clear head. *One drink would only steady your nerves.* I continued to stare at the wineskin and picked it up. How could I cherish something that had caused so much heartache? Just one drink could not hurt. I took a long drink and nearly ingested half of the wine that was there. You would think that through years of practice, I would be a master at rationing by now, but these days, it all seemed so random. Sometimes, I could empty my wineskin and be fine. On other days, it would be way too much and I would lose my self-control.

It made no sense to me, but I felt as though I needed the courage. Yahweh had not sent me any clear message, so I must not be a part of his plans. I took another little drink and put it back under the board where it had been hidden overnight. I decided that now was as good a time as any to start this new portion of my life.

I headed to the altar, for once not hating myself for entering this heathen building. I stood before the temple, somewhat fearful that yesterday would repeat itself. I had brought some wheat as an offering. If Yahweh would not speak to me, maybe Ba'al had some words of guidance. I entered the poorly lit temple and placed my offering at the base of the altar. I was thankful that nobody else was in there.

I looked at the grotesque statue and doubt rushed over me. I still felt a conviction that I should be with Padma, but all of a sudden, placing my future hopes in the hands of this creature did not seem like a viable option.

"Good morning, love." A voice whispered to me from behind.

I turned around and there sparkled Padma. She was just as beautiful as always. I couldn't suppress a smile at her greeting and stride towards her. "Good morning, my love." I kissed her gently. It felt as if it were the most natural thing in the world. It was a kiss that was meant to be shared each morning between two, lifelong companions. It was a clarifying action in a blurry world.

"Why are you here so early? Not that I am not happy to see you, of course." She said as our lips parted.

"I have come to invite you to my home today. I told my father about us and he is eager to meet you." Her smile vanished and she became visibly nervous.

"Your father knows about me?" She ended our embrace and stepped backward.

I must have had a confused look on my face because she looked away. "Of course. I had to tell him. If we are going to have a life together, he will inevitably be a part of it. Is that ok?" I said, fear starting to seep into my thoughts again.

"Of course." she stammered. "Does he know *about* me though?"

Her source of anxiety became clear at that moment. "He does not know everything about you. You can share with him only what you feel comfortable sharing. When I told him about us last night, you should have seen his face. I have not seen my father happy in many years. He was sincerely happy for us. I swear it."

She smiled again and a tear formed in the corner of her eye. "That is sweet of you to say."

"I only say it because it is the truth. This is a man who finds it hard to get up from the table or even put his drink down for a second, yet last night he was planning on where we would build our house on our property. By now, he has probably already determined how many children we are to bear. I tell you truthfully, without meeting you, you possibly have saved his life."

She laughed at the exaggerated sentiment but smiled serenely. "You are making fun of me."

I grabbed her gently, yet firmly by the shoulders, and made her look into my eyes. "I most sincerely am not. I believe that he already loves you without ever once having laid eyes upon you. You don't need to impress him. You just need to be yourself and I'm sure he will be happy again."

She embraced me again and I felt the relief of her soul. "I'm sure I can get away for a few minutes this afternoon. It does get pretty busy after the working day so I'll need to be back later in the day. Is that too short a time? Is it enough?"

The idea of my dad staying sober that far into the day was unlikely, so I found this to be a suitable timeline of the day. "It would be perfect. Do you want me to accompany you, or shall you just meet us there at the farm?"

"As much as it terrifies me to simply show up, I feel that is our best option. I don't want you to have to wait around for me to get an opportunity but I promise I will be there."

"I would wait a thousand days for you but I will go if you wish."

"I insist. I will be there as soon as I can."

I smiled and kissed her once more. I turned and walked away from the temple. It took everything I had inside of me not to run in excitement but I focused on each step and smiled absurdly at nothing. I must have looked like a complete imbecile on my walk home but I could offer no concerns over such issues. When I returned, my father was up and eating breakfast at the table.

I had been debating how to see if he had remembered the conversation from the day before but that was answered when I walked in the house. Of the three outfits he owned, he was wearing the nicest one that had not seen the light of day in quite some time. His hair was neatly combed and he actually had a clear look in his eyes.

When I entered, he looked up and smiled. "Is she visiting with us today?" His eagerness was almost too much to bear. My heart was bursting with boyish demeanor.

I smiled again, "She is. She will be here in a little while, as soon as she can get away."

"We must clean up, then." He got up and started towards the corner, where our kitchen was. I feared I would collapse from shock! My father was organizing the few dishes we had. Pots that had not hung on the wall for years were now placed gently upon hooks. This was going to be perfect. I knew it in my heart.

When everything was presentable, and after I had run a few errands to my shed, we sat at the table and talked. I was concerned that emotions would get the best of me from this unprecedented turn of events when a shadow spread across our floor.

There she was.

Padma stood in the door, her lovely brown hair curled and hanging down far beyond her shoulders. She had her blue dress on that had left him speechless the night before. She even held flowers in both hands at her waist in front of her. She looked incredibly nervous and we both stared for a few seconds before jumping to our feet.

"Come in. Please, come in." My father said breathlessly as he pulled a chair out for her to sit in. Padma finally let a smile show, dimples forming in her cheeks. I had never noticed them before. How had I never noticed them before? She stepped forward, towards the chair, still unsure of herself.

"Please forgive me for saying," My father started, "but you are the picture of beauty. You remind me so much of my wife." He stood frozen, enchanted by her.

Padma blushed and said, "Thank you, sir. I am honored to be a guest in your house."

"Honored?" My father dismissed the very notion and turned to me. "She said *she* is honored." The words were spoken in disbelief as he turned back to her. "It is I that am honored that you would bless this house with your presence. You are simply stunning." My father was in danger of rambling on and on so I decided to relieve him of his speaking duties.

"Padma, please sit down. You are most welcome in our home." She nodded and sat in the chair that was offered to her.

"This is such a lovely farm." She said, looking out the door into the fields. "There is so much space here. It is if the light touches everything. In the city, there are so many shadows. They hide the beauty that is all around us but here, you can see everything."

"It is just a modest farm, but I appreciate your sentiments." My father said. He remained standing until I sat and gave him a glare. He nodded an apology and sat with us. "It has been in my family for generations. It will never make us wealthy but it will always give us a place to rest our heads at night. There is also room to add more. There is flat land by our batch of grapes that would be perfect for another house. The sunrise here is an amazing sight. If you like open spaces, you will love it here. The fields stretch..."

"Yes. It is a modest farm, but the surroundings are quite spectacular to see." I said, cutting off my father. I believe he would have talked until someone stopped him. It was like he was a little boy again. I had never seen him like this before.

"Sorry. I don't get many visitors here. I did not mean to talk so much."

"I love to hear you talk. Please do not apologize to me." Padma said, smiling at him and melting my father's heart.

"Please, tell me about yourself."

At this, the color drained from Padma's face. She had to know that this question was coming, but apparently, had not found the answer yet.

"My history is very boring. I was orphaned by my parents at birth and never knew them." This statement was innocuous enough. This was common practice in cities like Rimmon.

"I'm so sorry to hear that. That is such a shame. Have you learned any trades to get by?"

Padma laughed nervously. "I'm afraid that I have not. I was left at a temple of Ba'al and that is where I have received most of my training." Padma and I both grew more nervous the closer we got to the absolute truth.

There were a couple of moments of awkward silence that filled the room. I knew that my father was adamantly against the worship of Ba'al so this would be a telling response that he was to offer. My father owned his Jewish heritage a little more than I did. Not much more, but I had a suspicion he still believed in Yahweh. The moment grew tense as my father leaned forward.

"I have found that a person's past is not nearly as important as their future. I am just glad that at this moment in time, you are here with us now." I was shocked and my mouth dropped open in surprise. The old man's fallibility had apparently led him to a place of humility that instantly became his greatest character trait. The conversation turned in every direction from there. By the time she left to go back to the temple, I had fallen in love with Padma all over again. I had also discovered a love for my father that had laid dormant for quite some time. It was the perfect afternoon. Maybe Yahweh had heard me after all.

Chapter Five

I am the artist of my own macabre sculpture. When given beautiful, deep, and vibrant colors to dabble in, I create a profound disaster that is only rivaled by armageddon. I watched Padma walk away from my home to return to the altar, life was finally right. We were to be husband and wife and own property and raise kids and end our days staring at the sunset discussing future plans. Those were the deep, vibrant colors I had to work with, but I can ruin the most beautiful of ingredients.

There's always a reason to drink. If you are celebrating or sad, there is an excuse. I was in a celebratory mood, so my mind instantly, no....violently shifted to wine. What better way to celebrate this perfect day than several glasses of wine?

I remember.

I remember embracing my father. An embrace that was long overdue. One that filled a part of my soul I had no idea was empty. It was glorious. He cried. Not in the way that old drunks do when reminiscing over lost opportunities and present failure. He cried tears of joy that hope had finally found a place to settle on our modest lot in the city of Rimmon in the region of Zebulun in the state of Israel.

I remember his pouring us a celebratory glass of wine and both of us acting like it wasn't a problem. After all, who wouldn't celebrate such an impending union with a glass of wine? It was normal. We pretended that we drank like normal people and our happiness increased.

I remember walking to Tabor's house. He would be skeptical of my plans with Padma but would never pass on the opportunity to drink in celebration with an old friend. He would drink to celebrate the blowing of the wind. That walk was phenomenal. I normally stumble my way through the day, but today I strode with purpose. Of course, I had begun to feel the effects of the wine but I was in complete control.

I remember the conversation that I had with Tabor when I arrived at his house.

"Hello, Ethan! How do you fare on this grand day?"

"Tabor, I have never been better a single moment in my life."

I remember that Ethan raised his eyebrows in surprise. "Well come in for a drink and tell me all about it!"

"Padma has met my father and we have decided that we shall be joined together in marriage. We will build a small abode, which I am sure you will help with, on our land and we will raise a family on that damned plot of land that has only given me despair and isolation. You will be a surrogate uncle to all of our little people and we will live in love and joy the rest of our days."

"As far as the surrogate uncle, I am all in. As far as the house-building, I'm sure Amos has all of the muscle that you need. I don't mean to spoil a good drink as if that were possible, but are you entirely sure that this is the best course of action for you? Not to be crude, but you....you could still have Padma without ridding yourself of the eligibility."

I remember acting offended at the statement despite owning that sentiment in my own head, "I have indeed considered every course of action. This is the decision that I feel most certain...no..proud of. I find myself giddy at the mere prospect of being the only man in Padma's life. She will never have to 'work' at that forsaken temple another day in her life. She will belong to me and I will treat her like the queen she was born to be. There are no words that you could string together that would convince me otherwise."

"That I should not dain to attempt such a contemptuous notion," I remember that Tabor raised his glass in cheers and we bumped our glasses together and finished our wine in one large gulp.

"We should celebrate such an occasion in regal style." I declared.

I remember that we both gathered ourselves and headed to our usual wine shop. The very location where so much of my directionless debauchery was staged should now serve as my altar of redemption. It made perfect sense in my liquid-addled brain.

I remember ordering our first round of drinks which elicited a cheer from the patrons sitting around us. I was patted on the back and congratulated multiple times as the wine flowed freely. These are memories that I shall grip in my lowest moments.

"Tell me, young Ethan. What is it about this woman that makes you feel the desire to take yourself off the open market, as they say?" Tabor asked while sipping his wine.

I remember looking at the floor and fighting back tears, thinking of how her simple touch was the only worship I ever felt compelled to perform. It was the only sensation I wished to feel for the rest of my days. She was all that I needed, wanted, or would pursue until I was buried in a cave somewhere in the Israeli hills, only to be mourned by my seven adult male children, several years down the road.

I had found what everyone ever birthed had ever sought. I would hold on to it with all that I had. I looked directly into Tabor's eyes and said, "I am hers and she is mine. A simple statement that belies the depth of unspeakable conviction. I can't explain what I know, I simply know it to be true."

Tabor almost looked jealous for a moment and nodded slowly. "Then explanatory measures would be a waste of our time. After all, when you are pursuing the rest of your life, why wait another minute? I had anticipated this moment and prepared a list of reasons to talk you out of it but I shall forever dispose of such idiocy and merely offer my sincerest of joyous sentiments to you and the blushing bride. I am happy for you, Ethan. The emptiness in a man's being is ever present in the eyes but it is absent from you for the first time since the day I met you. I could get used to this version of Ethan. In fact, I now shall insist upon this version of Ethan. He is a much better drinking partner than the old one."

I remember finishing a few more glasses of wine.

What occurred from that moment on, is a little less vivid. It still mystifies me why I can't just have a few glasses of wine like most people

I know and find solace in its warmth. Why do I so desperately seek the bottom of each glass that is set before me? Flashes of the evening urgently hasten my night.

We left the wine shop with the intention of finishing our celebration at the altar of Ba'al one last time.

I stumbled in the street on the way there. I remember that. Tabor and I laughed so hard it took more than a few moments to get me upright again.

I remember walking up the temple, still just a little fearful of what I would find.

I remember feeling disappointed when I could not find Padma anywhere.

I remember seeing Dabria, her bewitching smile adorning her face, as she walked towards us with a bedazzling look in her eyes.

"What brings you two handsome men to a place like this?" She asked as she placed her hands on our shoulders. I remember being stirred by the touch and instantly hating myself for the response. I looked away and let Tabor do the talking.

"Have you not heard? Our friend here is engaged to be married. He will forever be taken in the eyes of the gods under the banner of heaven." Tabor said in reply. I remember we all giggled a bit as he slurred his words. If Tabor was inebriated, that meant I was way beyond help. He always handled his wine better than I did and we had had the same amount by my inebriated estimation.

"I have heard and it appears that the celebration has already started!" Dabria said as she leaned in for a kiss from Tabor.

"It has, indeed. It is now the hour in which you join the party that has long started." Tabor said with a devilish look in his eyes. Dabria returned the look until I interrupted.

"Where is Padma?" I said, wobbling back and forth just a little.

Dabria chuckled, "I'm not sure if you'd even notice her if she was here."

I remember being slightly irritated at the statement, as well as frustrated by not receiving a response. "Where is Padma?" I uttered again, embarrassed by my words and actions.

I remember....barely...Dabria turned her full attention to me and put both hands on my arms, her eyes, and invitation, her lips an unexpected and sudden lure. "She is not here. She has left for a client and vowed that she will not be back."

"I don't understand...." I slurred. Dabria inched closer to me and Tabor moved behind her.

"Yes, you do." Has everything been a lie? Had I misread the situation so completely that I now had to stand here, completely lost and humiliated?

I remember her lips touching mine.

I was thankful that I remembered nothing else.

Chapter Six

Consciousness evaded me for quite some time. There were vague blurs that were indistinguishable between reality and fevered dream. Dabria hovered above me, unclothed, helping me sip wine from a jug. I lay hunched in a corner, emptying my stomach violently. Sunshine and the dead of the night seemed to take turns, randomly through the doors and windows. I know that exposure in my state should have heaped shame upon me, but in my delirious mind, I simply willed myself to focus on staying alive and breathing.

The only thing worse than being in an awakened state was deep slumber. There, nightmares could run amok unchecked. I lay on the cold, stone floor, surrounded by nothing. When I say nothing, I mean the complete absence of any recognizable setting. The 'nothingness' was black and foreboding. It seemed to crawl towards me at every side. In that nothingness lay death and finality that was indescribably terrifying. The blackness held a death in it that screamed nothing lay beyond. No Yahweh. No Ba'al. Just a devoid, oblivious being. I lay powerless to move. Tears streamed down my eyes, complete sadness at the demise of what was probably once a promising existence.

So much potential, laying inebriated in a faux brothel disguised as a place of worship. There was so much more beyond the darkness that had not invited me. If it had, the invitation was long lost. I never knew that squandered opportunity actually could leave a taste in your mouth and it was bitter and reeked of vomit.

Dabria again with the wine. Another round of sunlight and dead of night. Sensations came and went, but I stayed in the same, prone position. I was useful to no one but worse, I could not stir enough concern within me to act on any instinct. At one point, I felt a tingle in my chest. The more my mind focused on that tingle, the more it felt like a tiny insect desperately trying to devour its way out of my body. It multiplied, garnering more support for this violent uprising against my corporeal being. Thousands of bugs within me, attempting a frenzied escape that threatened to tear me apart from the inside. Once it felt as if they were about to breach the skin, I finally jolted upright in a state of panic. The early morning sun had apparently just started to stream in through the doors and windows. Unfortunately, this was a familiar scene. I looked around the altar where I remember my descent into the abyss began.

There was no one here.

I faintly remembered screams and the acrid smell of fire, but that could have easily been associated with one of the many night terrors, or in my case, day terrors. I set my sweaty palm down on the cool floor and used my other hand to wipe the sweat from my forehead. I had woken up in this setting many times, covered in a sheer glaze of shame, but others had always been strewn about this den of sin. Today, I was alone. More alone than I had ever felt before. I stayed in this position for about thirty minutes, unsure of how to proceed with my day, not pressured to escape under the night sky because of waking cohorts.

It surprised me when I started crying. The dream about being surrounded by an encroaching empty crevasse was all too real, even now in the sanctity of awareness. I was nothing. I would always be nothing. Any hope that young Ethan had carried with him into this world had long vanished.

My head throbbed from what I could only assume was a multiple-day binge of wine and my back ached from the stone flooring. The thought of standing up was so intimidating that it took four or five attempts to finally make it to my feet. I wobbled a bit and began to feel my heart race. Had I done some permanent damage? I stepped forward and dizziness washed over me. I felt my hands trembling and looked around the room for more wine.

What madness! Wine brought me here. Wine kept me here and wine had put me in this state yet it was the first thing I thought of when trying to escape. I told myself that if I could actually make it home, I would then reward myself with a drink.

Then, the memory of Padma struck me like a sword across the chest. I wobbled again. She had chosen life with another man. Just when everything had fallen into place, it had been ripped cruelly away from me. She had never mentioned any of the other 'worshippers' by name but I could easily see someone with more status whisking her away. All I had to offer her was a poor farm and a tiny one-room house. I should have known better.

I stepped outside and tried to wipe the sweat and tears away and immediately noticed that everything was different. No one was on the street and for that, I was thankful. An eeriness filled the air and I slowly stumbled forward. Smoke filled the streets and burned my eyes, which triggered the tears all over again. I noticed a house on the side of the street, demolished down to rubble. Several more buildings appeared in the same state.

What had happened while I was out? I inched my way forward and noticed a man lying on the side of one of the houses that had been destroyed. I made my way over to him and found him staring into the sky, dead to this world. Blood streamed from his temples and I leaned forward and threw up on the ground next to him. I backed away, terror starting to trickle into my mind. I saw a couple of other people lying on the ground as well. One was a small child. I didn't dare check on them. Shame filled my soul but I had no stomach for such happenings this morning. I began to pick up my pace as blood flow was restored to my limbs. I had to make it home. I needed a drink now more than I did just moments before.

I stopped along the way and emptied the contents of my stomach once more. The farther away from the city of Rimmon, the more smoke filled the air. I passed one farm and the fields were completely engulfed in flames. I passed Lachlan's farm and it was in the same state. He had been a family friend before apparently giving up on my father. I stopped in front of the house and looked for him. Dread filled me as I saw his body laying on the ground. His arms were three to four feet away from his body which was laying in a lake of blood.

More tears streamed from my eyes and for the first time, it occurred to me to worry about my own home, my father! I started to run and every muscle in my body tried to resist. My legs burned as I sprinted down the dirt path. I felt empty, a strong desire to pray but no one to pray to. I saw flames along every horizon and panic settled in my throat. I thought I would pass out before reaching my homestead but I was doomed to see what had been done. I came upon my land and the silhouette of my house now had been reduced to a pile of rocks. Everything was gone.

The crops lay in smoldering ash and there were no goats to be seen. I stood, paralyzed by the weight of a depression that threatened to suffocate me. I openly wept.

I had nothing left.

I ran to the rubble that was my house hoping that my father had gone into town to buy more wine when all of this happened. He wouldn't be here. The other farmers had been slaughtered in their fields. I had seen no bodies on our land. I threw rocks aside, trying to get to the bottom of the pile to see if there was anything there that was salvageable. While removing a particularly large stone, I saw a hand and knew that my father was gone. My sight was blurry and nothing made sense. I kept digging to reveal his body. He had had his throat slit and I wept harder.

My only hope was that it had been a quick death, preferably while he was sleeping. My body shook with sobs as I leaned down to kiss his forehead. My tears dripped onto his face as I picked his upper body up and held it to my chest. He had been a flawed man, but he was my father. He was the only person on this earth who loved me unconditionally. I worked for another hour to reveal the rest of his body and removed him from the pile of ash-stained stone. As I pulled him free, I noticed a leg. It made no sense to me. I looked down at my father again to make sure he had all of his limbs. He did.

The leg was not his and confusion replaced the crushing despair that had previously resided within me. I furiously began digging in the rubble to reveal who the leg belonged to. My father had never courted another woman after the death of my mother so this was truly unfathomable. It wasn't until I had removed the final few blocks that I realized who it was.

Padma.

I stared at her through my tears, utterly lost. Why had Padma come here? It made no sense at all. The whole world had fallen apart as I lay wasted beside a false altar. Then, Dabria's words came back to me.

"She is not here. She has left for a client and vowed that she will not be back."

I had been the client that she had left for.

Why had Dabria refused to reveal this information to me?

Why had Dabria seduced me when she must have known that Padma left, *for me?*

I held her tightly to my chest and cried even harder. Now, I have truly lost everything. I could do nothing but cry on my knees, among the two dead bodies that I loved the most. I fell asleep without concern that the men who had done this could still be in the region. I had no regard for my life. If they come back, let them finish the job. I would not even put up a fight. In fact, I would beg for the end that I so desperately craved.

* * * * *

I fought the urge to do nothing and without thought, buried Padma and my father amongst the fields where the goats had once grazed. It took me two days and all of the strength that I had. I only stopped for water and to cry. My biggest fear was that someone would see me. I was in no mood for company and had already made a plan for my next move.

Once the burial was done, I found what few possessions remained and packed them up. I did not have any additional clothes to change into and the linens that I wore were stained with blood, vomit, tears, ash, and dirt. My face and arms were covered with the same. I must have been a sight to see but I was lucky in the sense that no one had approached the farm. After all, my father had inadvertently squandered any friendships long ago, of course, no one would come to check on our safety.

I tied my knife to my side and headed for the caves among the hills of Rimmon. I did not travel the main roads and cut through the pomegranate grove where I had confessed my love for Padma. I had apparently expunged all of the liquid from my body because no tears fell anymore. I was simply devoid of any emotion at all. Hopelessness was the only thing I felt. With it, a sense of relief. I had no expectations of this life anymore. I had squandered any chances I might have had and there was no one left to look after me.

I came to the conclusion that the Midianites had engaged in another raid and that my house was conveniently in their way. I took some consolation that my farm would not have been rich plunder for them. I hope they stung with disappointment when they saw what little possessions lie in my house.

The closer I got to the caves, I finally started to see people stirring. We avoided eye contact as I settled into an empty cave to wallow in isolation and self-pity. In my peripheral vision, I surmised that they were in a similar situation as me. Families destroyed by senseless violence. I stared out of the cavern entrance, scanning a view that would have otherwise been impressive. Now it was just a front-row seat to plumes of smoke along the countryside. My father and future wife were dead because I had had too much to drink. There was no forgiveness for a man like me. I was beyond redemption. I looked down at the knife in my hand. It had been dull from use but was plenty sharp enough to complete one last job.

Since I was a master at procrastination, I determined that I would sleep here tonight and finish the job in the morning. Then, if any of the gods had ever been real, I would see Padma and my father by the time night fell tomorrow.

Chapter Seven

Nightmares riddled my attempt at slumber as soon as I closed my eyes. A disturbing, heart-wrenching collision of scenarios played out in my head featuring my father and Padma. The encroaching void made an appearance as well and I woke often with fresh tears streaming down my face. At some point in the night, when exhaustion overwhelmed me, I found sweet relief. The idea of waking in the morning and taking my own life gave me a respite that seemed to calm my spirit.

Amos had his soldier friends and Tabor had his drinking buddies, so I was relatively sure that no one would give a second thought to the news of a former friend being found dead in a cave outside of Rimmon. They would understand. No one could, or should, endure the losses that I had to bear. The recurring desire for liquid courage kept bubbling up inside of me but I had no means of acquiring some so I would have to engage in my final performance in complete sobriety. Would I be brave enough to make one last, bold statement?

Finally, the early dawn sunlight streamed through the threadbare clouds and made its way to my eyes. Free from feeling the effects of over-indulgence, I was able to open my eyes and not spend the first few minutes of my day replaying the night's events in my head. Nothing could stop the last few day's tragic events from visiting, but my mind was broken and I had become completely numb. I propped myself up on the cool stone floor and looked around.

I took out my hunting knife and held it to my throat. I was loath to any sort of violence but I would have to find the will to perform this brutal, expedient act and relief would follow. Sure, I was not looking forward to the pain, but it would be as brief as it was intense. I took the tip of the knife and held it just to the left of my jugular and started to push. Harder and harder, but with a cowardly slowness. I pushed. I felt blood rush from my neck. I knew that I would have to keep at it to get the job done so I forced myself to keep the pressure increasing.

What happened next was a confusion of blurry images. I remember lying back, blood pouring from my neck, and then I remember seeing the silhouette of an angel. I had done it! I was still unsure how I had merited an angel upon my departure from this world, but I felt the hands as surely as anything else I had ever experienced. I knew that my eyes were still open but blackness filled my field of vision like a converging circle.

I felt the knife fall to the ground and heard a distant clacking at its landing. Impossibly, someone appeared before me just before the blackness filled my purview.

That couldn't be right. I was aware enough to know that other people had inhabited caves around me, but my own personal tomb was not visible to them. I did not make a sound so they would not attempt any intervening actions. The timing of this visit was tragic. I felt pressure on my neck where the knife had entered and cloth or linen was applied harshly. I knew the man was saying something but it seemed so far away and much too unimportant to listen to. My legs went painfully numb and my arms followed as my head seemed to float away. How long would it take to bleed out? This was surprisingly painful yet relieving pain. I convinced myself that the more the pain flowed through my body the closer I was to either the next world or oblivion. Either way is preferable to the promises made by this earth and its misery.

It was at that point that I lost consciousness and welcomed my next destination.

* * * * *

There was no way for me to measure time, but I could feel that a large amount had passed before I gathered myself enough to stir. I did not know if I was dead or alive, but I was sure I had never experienced such full-body pain before. Every inch of my body, inside and out, pulsated with a dull, aching agony that filled me with a strong urge to scream.

Of course, that would have necessitated far too much energy and I was dreadfully short of that right now.

I wanted to open my eyes but was more than a little fearful of what I would see. There was a part of me that wanted to see the cave where I had put the knife to my neck, to try again and rebuild a life worthy of being proud of. There was another part of me that wanted to see what the afterlife actually looked like. Of course, I had imagined that the afterlife was free of physical pain, so I doubted that I was there.

I slowly lifted the lids of my eyes and sunlight began to stream in. Memories of waking up at the altar on so many occasions rushed back into my mind. Why was waking up such a monumental task for me? *Because you always choose to end your day in utter debauchery!* I heard myself chastise.

The man who I had seen rush into my grotto as I descended into the darkness was sitting before me, staring out at the sky and all it had to offer. He had not been a vision unless I was still hallucinating. I tried to push myself up and this apparently startled the man. He turned and looked at me as I tried to sit up.

"My God - you look so pale!" He gasped.

"Forgive me..." I tried to say more but the pain in my throat was searing.

The man reached out as if to stop me from talking. "I wouldn't say anything if I were you."

Thanks for that advice I thought with rancor.

"You were lucky that I arrived when I did. If I had even been a few seconds later, I imagine you would have accomplished what you set out to do." He said as he helped me sit. My head swam and everything seemed to waver. I was nauseous and worried that I might vomit, but then I remembered that I had not eaten anything in days.

Linen had been tied to the wound in my neck and I put my hand there to steady it as I tried to speak once more. "Why?"

"Why? Why did I stop you?" The man looked genuinely confused. He was about my age and had curly brown hair. His large, hazel eyes transfixed on mine, wondering if I was serious.

"Yes." I said, trying to hold my neck still as I talked.

The man thought for a second. "If you would have asked me in the moment, I would have said it was out of instinct. But now that I have had plenty of time to ponder that query, I would say that it was through divine intervention."

My confusion at this revelation was obviously transparent because it prompted him to explain more.

"You see, I am on a mission; a mission from Yahweh himself." The man looked down at the cavern floor for a second, almost embarrassed. "I know how that sounds. It must seem like insanity to you, but I assure you it is not. There is a man named Jerubbaal. He has been informed by God that he is to destroy the Midianites. Can you imagine that? Could you imagine how profound, how powerful that would be - to actually hear the word of God?"

The man was overcome with passion and I completely believed that he believed that. I, on the other hand, was simply focusing on each breath. Contemplating the communication patterns of deities was not my top priority at the moment.

"How does..." I started and had to take a deep breath. "That impact me?" I asked. Does some guy hear a voice and another one shows up to ruin my plans? I couldn't quite make the connection between the two events.

"Gideon has sent messengers out to the children of Israel to ask them to come to fight for him. Victory over the Midianites is guaranteed with God on our side and who would not want the honor and glory that comes from ridding the earth of those heathens? Anyway, I am one of the messengers and had heard that the Midianites had raided the area a short time ago and figured there would be some Israelites here that might want to get revenge. Of course, I didn't expect to see someone trying to take their own life, but I figured God put you in my path for a reason. I didn't want to sit around and wait for you to wake up at first. I am in a hurry to get as many people as I can, but after a while, I figured that God might want you and it would be a sin to just leave you here to die."

I laughed in spite of myself, which sent another round of torment through my limbs and throat. I pressed hard on my neck and talked as softly as I could. "So, your story is that you were sent by God to round up soldiers to fight a war and you looked at me, alone and bleeding to death in a cave, and thought 'He'd make a good soldier?'"

He laughed as well and countered, "Well, yeah. At least I know you are good with a knife."

We both smiled and I shook my head. I liked this man instantly. "What is your name?"

"I am Rafal. I am of the tribe of Benjamin."

"I am Ethan. It is a pleasure to meet you, Rafal." I said, meaning each word I spoke. "I wish that I saw what you saw, but alas, I am not a soldier. What you saw was my last attempt to use a knife in any way, shape or form. I could not even kill a willing participant, let alone one who resists such advances."

Rafal's expression donned a somber tone as he turned to face me. He looked deep into my eyes to make me feel what he said next, "It is not important what I see. It only matters what the great and glorious Yahweh sees and he does not make mistakes. He finds people wherever they happen to be and he lifts them up for His glory. I don't know your story. I don't know your history. I do know my God, though and to proclaim that he can not use you is nothing less than blasphemy! I can't force you to walk the path that he has laid out before you, nor would I choose to if I could, but believe me when I say, it is your path."

It was my turn to look down at the cavern floor in shame. His words rippled through my very being and I was surprised to find tears beginning to form in the corners of my eyes. No one ever told me that

I could be part of something so profound. The closest I had ever been to being a part of something truly special was with Padma, and she was now lost to me forever.

Rafal continued, "I assume that you are not in the best chapter of your story, but I can assure you it's not the last chapter. I urge you to fight. If it is alongside of me, fighting for Jerubbaal, so be it. If it is fighting to get up and leave this self-made tomb, that works as well. But you need to fight nonetheless. Your future self deserves the effort!"

That did it. A tear streamed down my cheek and I wiped it away quickly. I knew that he was right. Of course, I had no idea what to do next but I suddenly knew I had to live. I nodded my head in agreement and tried to speak. No words came out because of the lump in my throat. I was so tired. If conversation could incite this exhaustion within me, how was I to join an army and take vengeance on the same people who had taken everything from me?

"My mission is not complete. I feel that God wants me to continue on but I will tell you that it was a pleasure to meet you, Ethan. If you feel that your path lies with the righteous, you are to meet in Shunem, east of Meggido. It is not too far from here."

"Thank you, Rafal. Thank you for everything." I nodded to him in appreciation. He had saved my life twice. With that, he was up on his feet.

"May God watch over you and keep you safe." He turned and exited the cave and I leaned back against the wall of the cave and took a deep breath. I pondered what my next move would be. I had land to return to, but no home. I had memories but no family. I had youth and strength but no real skill to earn an honest living. On the other hand, I had never been outside of Rimmon and the thought of seeing other parts of Israel could be invigorating.

In that defining moment, I decided that I would seek out Amos and talk to him of this recent revelation. He would know what to do. I would fight. What I would fight, I could not tell you, but I would fight.

Chapter 8

I did not fight that day. As deep as my motivation was when Rafal left, other forces were equally strong in the aftermath. I tried several times to get up but found the activity far too taxing for any semblance of longevity or momentum. I found it easier to lay there, imagining fighting in the future. It took another day before I was steady enough on my feet to make it back to Rimmon. It looked much the same as when I left it. The smoke plumes were mostly gone now, but the destruction was still evident.

I avoided going by the temple, fearing that I would see Dabria. The fury that I felt towards her was palpable and I didn't know what I would say. I had to avoid Tabor's house as well. I felt vague anger towards him as well but could not put the finger on why. He had not forced me to that altar that night. He was not the reason I wasn't home to protect and save my family. Those were choices that I had made. That realization was what filled me with shame as I stood outside the wine shop.

It was the wine that had kept me from being beside Padma and my father, yet here I was again, longing for just one more drink. I rationalized that it could also be the reason I was still alive today. If I had not over-indulged, I would have just gone home that night and the Midianites would have slaughtered me as well.

I walked into the shop, and shame and excited anticipation danced inside of me. I was thankful that Tabor was not there, for I was in no mood to talk. Even if I was, I would have no idea what to say to him. I ordered my drink with the promise that I had family coming into town later and they would pay for me. This was, of course, a lie. I had no family left. As soon as I took the first drink, any hesitation I held onto seemed to dissipate. With wine in my belly, I believed that the world was an opportunity and that I would take full advantage of it.

Just then, I felt a hand on my shoulder. I turned to see who it was and pain shot through my neck again. I feared that I had opened the wound and instantly reached up to see if I was bleeding.

"How are you feeling, friend?" Tabor said as he emerged from behind me and sat where he normally did. He had a drink in hand but was too busy inspecting me to pay attention to it. His face revealed his concern for me. It was an odd expression for Tabor. He was usually jovial and full of spirit. Now, he just looked scared.

"I'll be ok." I said, still holding my neck and talking softly.

"What happened to you? Was it the Midianites?"

I marinated on the question a bit. I did not want to go into the details of my suicidal adventure and decided that it was just easier to go with his assumption.

"Yes, I ran into a couple on my land...it's a long story." I had neither the energy nor the desire to construct an entire tale so I just left it at that and hoped that he would not ask any further questions.

"You don't look so good, but I am thankful you are alive."

I offered a short, curt laugh and took another drink. It occurred to me that I had not wondered about Tabor's state of affairs. Leave it to me to be swallowed up in my own drama, with no concern for anyone else.

"How are you and your family?" I asked nervously, unaware if they had been affected by the raid.

"The house and farm are destroyed but my family is safe. We were able to flee just in time but had to watch from a distance as they burned or stole everything we had ever owned. He looked down and took a drink for himself. I had never seen him so melancholy before.

I thought about his comment for a moment and it confused me a bit. "How did you make it home in time to save your family? You were at the temple with me."

Guilt spread over his face and he looked behind me in an attempt to avoid eye contact. "One of the girls from the temple heard that the raid was coming. I was awakened by this news early in the morning. You had just fallen asleep. I tried to wake you up, but there was nothing I could do."

Anger rose up from my stomach and I felt my face turn red. I knew that I had to be careful and not let emotions dictate my words but at the moment, I did not care. "So Dabria just kept feeding me wine while you saved your family and mine was slaughtered?" The words came out quickly and louder than I wanted them to. My throat ached but as long as the wound stayed closed, I could handle it.

"I got my family to safety and returned to you as soon as I could. Once I had heard about what happened to your father and Padma..." He looked at the floor again and shame prevented him from continuing.

"You abandoned me?"

"I told Dabria to keep you drunk so that you would be safe. At that point, there was nothing you could have done and I just wanted to keep you alive. It may not have been the best decision I ever made but I stand by it."

I put my hand over my face and rubbed my temples. I took a deep breath and tried to make sense of all that had happened. Could they really have acted out of good intentions? Tabor had been a good friend if not a bad influence but he would never want to see me harmed. Anger is sometimes hard to erase but it was definitely starting to dim.

"I understand." I said, which was partially a lie. "What are you going to do now?"

"Pay for your drink and have another. It is all I can think to do. I know that we have to rebuild, but I sure don't want to start now."

"Thank you for the drink. I wasn't sure how I was going to pay for it."

"No problem," Tabor said as he ordered another round. "What do you plan to do?"

I thought for a moment. How would I even begin to try and explain what had happened the past couple of days? I finally decided that I would give him a slightly modified version of the story and leave out all that 'killing myself' nonsense.

"After the attack, I fled to some caves outside Rimmon and slept there for a couple of nights. I met a man who was recruiting for an army of some sort. He said I was welcome to join them and fight the Midianites. At this moment, that seems like the best, if not my only, course of action. I came back to town to talk to Amos about it."

I expected Tabor to dismiss the idea as a complete absurdity. He did not strike me as someone who could adhere to authority. He was also adamantly against violence. So his response shocked me to my very core. "Can anyone join?"

I looked up, eyes wide. "Are you serious right now? You want to become a soldier?"

There was no hint of good humor in his eyes and with all sincerity, he said, "Why not? What do I have to look forward to here? My family is safe but I'm not tied to them. I have no woman in my life to marry. I'm not sure marriage is even a goal of mine anyway."

"I can't believe what I am hearing. That is the last path that I would imagine you choosing. I mean no offense, of course." I could see that my surprise had stung him a bit.

"If I did choose to do it, it would be to make sure you don't stab yourself and die. Someone has to keep an eye on you." He could not realize how close to home his words hit but I faked a smile rather than go into it.

"I'm not completely convinced it is what I am going to do, but I just don't see any other options." I said as I finished my second drink, feeling better than I had in days.

"Well, let's go talk to Amos and see what the big guy has to say about it."

I looked around the room, wondering if there was an elaborate prank being played on me. "You want to go talk to Amos?"

"As I've said before, I actually do have a fondness for the man, even if he abhors my company." Tabor said with a smile finally spreading across his face. For a brief moment, life seemed normal again. Wine can bring moments like that, but they are often fleeting. Wine can also stir memories that you wish to stay hidden from the light of day. Those have a habit of popping up moments after elation and peace.

It then occurred to me that I could not visit Padma at the end of this current binge and my heart broke all over again. I wished to not dwell on this moment any longer so I forced myself back into the conversation. "As long as you play nice with Amos," I said as I finished my drink and stood up slowly.

"Always. Off we go."

Chapter Nine

Anxiety started to swirl around in my head and caused my knees to buckle as I approached the shelter where Amos stayed. What was I thinking? A couple of days ago, I was planning on spending the rest of my days on my homestead with my wife, and now I was contemplating on going to war, *as a soldier,* for a cause I was still uncertain of.

I remembered that this war was against the people who had foiled my earlier plans but that did not make me a soldier. I stopped briefly and Tabor put his hand on my shoulders.

"Are you sure about this?" He said with a tenderness that was so foreign from him that I now doubted myself even more.

"I'm not sure about any of this. Are you sure about this?"

Tabor looked from Amos' residence to my eyes, "I'm not sure either, but I feel an excitement deep inside me that I haven't felt for quite some time. It might be worth a shot." I stared at Tabor. I barely recognized my lifelong friend and his seemingly new persona, but it did steady me a bit.

"We will just have a talk and see where it leads." I said, still willing to evacuate the plan at the first opportunity presented to me.

We walked up and Amos was leaving through the opening. He seemed surprised to see us, especially Tabor. "Ethan. How are you?" He said, completely ignoring the fact Tabor was standing beside me. I must have still looked horrendous because he was gawking at me as if I was a walking corpse.

"I'm doing alright. I've had a rough couple of days." I said modestly.

Amos dropped his head and said sympathetically, "I heard about your father. You have my sympathies. I came to call on you yesterday but could not find you. Needless to say, I was gravely concerned. Is there anything that I can do?"

I was thankful that he did not bring up my current condition because I didn't want to go through my lie again, especially with Amos. "I was wondering if we could talk for a moment."

"Hi, Amos. It is good to see you again." Tabor said, forcing his way into the conversation.

Amos begrudgingly looked at Tabor and nodded. He sensed that this was not a good time to revisit past resentments.

"Of course. Come in." We walked into the dark shelter that was only lit by two small windows. It was a humble abode that only had a couple of pots and jars set by a small bed that covered the floor in the corner. We sat down on the floor and we took the water that was offered to us. It would have been nicer if wine were in the flasks, but water would do for now.

I began my abridged version of the story I had lived the past couple of days. "I was hiding in the caves outside Rimmon when I met a man named Rafal." I paused to see if Amos would recognize the name. That would have possibly made this decision easier, one way or the other, but he said nothing and I took the cue to continue. "He said that he was a messenger for that man Jerubbaal you told me about. He told us to meet east of Meggido, in a town called Shenum. There, Jerubbaal is gathering an army to fight the Midianites."

Amos nodded, "I have heard many good things about this Jerubbaal. He has risen to power alongside Deborah in this matter of ridding our land of these heathens. What is it you wish to talk to me about?"

Without my permission, a tear formed in my eye as I continued on, "I have nothing left, friend. The only family that I have ever known has been taken from me. The way that this messenger talked, stirred something in me. He looked at me. He looked at ME and decided that I would fit in with this growing force. Who looks at me and declares that I am honorable enough to fight for such a noble cause? Anyway, I guess it comes down to the fact that I just needed your advice on the matter."

Amos looked down in serious consideration and looked up at Tabor. "What is your part in all of this?"

"Tabor swallowed his water and coughed a bit, surprised to be included in the dialogue. "I am here to support my friend."

"Support him all the way to the battlefield?" Amos questioned.

"If that is what is necessary. Do you not think it is inside this heathen to hold such regard for friendship?" Tabor said, genuinely offended. It was just yet another example of a long line of reactions that stunned me.

"I will admit, your dedication is a surprise to me, but I am impressed. That is, if you do choose this path to go down." Amos said, softening his expression just a bit.

"I don't know a lot about such matters, but I do know that your closest friend is sitting here, mired in torment, seeking sound advice so I am eager to hear what your response will be."

Amos turned back to me, "So you are asking if you should join Jerubbaal in the fight against the Midianites?"

"That is indeed what I am asking." I said. This was a topic that was hard enough to broach, let alone beg for. I simply needed a clear, inspiring statement either supporting the action or dissuading me. Instead, I was met with prolonged silence. Amos bowed his head and placed his hands together. It took me a moment to realize that he was praying. His lips began to move and he spoke. His words were low and soft and indistinguishable to my ears. I longed to hear what his prayer sounded like. If I were to go on this journey, I would need a lot of prayers. Hearing an example of how to talk to this God would be helpful to me in the future. Apparently, it was too personal to include me.

I stared at Amos while he engaged in his spiritual conversation. In the corner of my eye, I saw Tabor turn and look at me but I didn't return the gaze. I was captivated by Amos. The conversation lasted a couple of minutes and finally, Amos raised his head. He pushed himself up from the ground and grabbed our flasks to return them to his pile of possessions.

"When you ask for advice that you are truly invested in hearing, the answer can be hard, confusing, and painful. Are you sure you wish to seek my counsel on such matters?"

"That is why I am here." I said in exasperation.

"I believe that you should go. In fact, if you choose to follow this path, I will go with you."

The response should not have surprised me but it did. I came to Amos because of his spiritual connection so his support of Jerubbaal should have been obvious. What surprised me was his willingness to go with me. I sat in the caves of Rimmon, ready to take my life because I assumed I had no one in this world that would care rather I lived or died. Now I sat in the presence of two men who were willing to literally go to war with me. It was a notion that I was not emotionally prepared for.

"Why do you believe I should go?" I said, truly wanting to know the answer.

"Ethan, you have endured something that has obviously changed you in some way. It would have changed anyone who has been through what you have. There is an opportunity for you to find your purpose on this earth. If a friend is not willing to go on that journey with you, he is no friend at all. I had planned to return to Deborah and fight alongside her, for she is leading a similar charge, but this changes everything."

"What if I am not ready for this? What if I am not good enough?" I heard my words, drenched in pity, as they left my mouth but it was truly what I feared.

"Our Creator is good. Our God loves you. He does not love you because of who you are, He loves you because of who He is. He has sent you a message, a call to action. He would not call you to see you fail.

You are destined to honor and glorify Him. I do not say this lightly. It is not simply a reaction to your question. I believe this. I do not stand before you as your judge, but I do have to ask you a question. Were you happy before the Midianites came?"

I furrowed my brow. "What do you mean?"

"I mean before you lost your father, were you happy in the life that you were pursuing?"

The difference between Amos and me was that he prayerfully answered questions posed to him whereas I simply responded, often with no thought. "I came and went as I pleased. I loved a woman with all of my heart. I..."

"That is not what I asked. I agree with your assessment of your life. You drank as much as you wanted. You sought love outside of the condition of marriage. You lived for yourself at any given moment of the day. Again, no judgment from me, but were you happy?"

Tabor shifted uncomfortably and I stopped my rambling brain to think. "I was not. I was pursuing things that left me empty inside but I did truly love Padma, despite my maudlin existence." I said in my defense. I might not have led the most moral life, but I was not going to let anyone, even my best friend, tell me that my love for Padma was sinful by nature.

"I'm not saying you did not love that woman, but did you pursue her in a way that you were proud of?"

I dropped my gaze to the floor. It was exhausting verbally sparring with Amos. He seemed to always argue from a position of power. He was right and I knew it. "I did not."

"Then honor her now with righteous pursuits. Yahweh has a plan for you and it does not include waking up in the house of Ba'al, still intoxicated from the night before. You have an opportunity to be a part of something that will stand the test of time. With all of my heart and soul, I believe that you should chase after this opportunity with all that you have. I promise to be by your side for every step of the journey. Even if that includes me having to spend more time with Tabor." In the most surprising turn of events that day, a small smile crossed Amos' lips. Even Tabor laughed under his breath a bit when he saw the expression on Amos' face.

"I will try to talk as little as possible." Tabor said jovially.

"Lies!" Amos said, smiling more broadly now, "but I will go anyway. What is better than one person finding salvation? Two. Let us go meet this Jerubbaal. If he finds us worthy, we will join him in battle and see victory before the Lord. The death and destruction that the Midianites have reigned upon our people will be rectified and we will live our lives in a way that is pleasing to the Lord."

My heart raced as I joined my friends in smiling. Amos put his arms around us and bowed his head again. He started to pray and I listened intently. He prayed for our safety. He prayed for our vision and our intentions. He prayed a prayer that filled me with hope.

I was going to be a soldier.

I would honor my father, and Padma's, memory.

I would finally find peace in my stormy soul.

I had no idea what to expect next.

Chapter Ten

My next order of business was not in accordance with my vision of the future but was vital in my mind. I told Tabor and Amos that I was going to "settle some affairs" and meet them back here to start our journey. I'm sure that my excuse was transparent, but both were kind enough not to comment. Amos just nodded solemnly and Tabor echoed my sentiment.

"What affairs does a man in your situation have to settle?" Tabor asked as we ventured from Amos' shelter.

"I am going to sell my property. It is of no use to me now and I wish to get something for it." I said with shame.

"That's fair. Do you think you might want to wait and make this decision with a clear head? You have no idea what lies in front of us."

I stopped and looked around. I drew in a deep breath and was paralyzed by doubt. I had no idea what to do next. I know I needed a supply of wine for this journey but no means to acquire it. Saying this out loud to Tabor was out of the question. It was shameful enough to think about it let alone give voice to it.

"What do we do next?" I said to Tabor, hoping he would know what to do.

"Well, we do need travel supplies. I can cover the expense now and if you still want to sell your land when we get back..."

"If we get back." I said, defeated.

"When we get back, you can settle that debt however you see fit."

I looked at Tabor with admiration. I had always considered him the worst side of me, but here he was, coming to my rescue with the best of intentions. I had misjudged him greatly.

"Let's get some refreshments for our journey and be on our way. Great things lie ahead, my friend. I feel it. For the first time in a long time, I feel it." Tabor said with his hand on my shoulder.

"I wished I shared your optimism." I said, thankful he understood my intention.

"That is what friends are for. When you are feeling the weight of the world, I will carry it for you. Soon, I will have a burden for you to bear and I'm sure you will be there to help me through it. As long as one of us has hope, we are unstoppable."

I smiled at him and we walked towards the wine shop. All I had with me was a sack that had once held grain, a jug, and a flask that had not been discovered by the Midianites.

"I have nothing that I can offer you at this point," I informed Tabor.

"It is of no consequence. I was able to stow away an extra jug and blanket for you. That should get us started.

The following hours were a wondrous display of Tabor's ingenuity. In his dealings with local merchants, he was able to use his charm and bartering skills to secure a large amount of wine, which was all I cared about, an extra wool tunic for me, since I had no spare clothing, dried dates, and figs, and a couple of salted fish that would last for the duration of our journey. Our most prized possession came through thievery though. I am not proud of this, it is a simple fact. Amongst the ruins of one of the Midianite's targets, we were able to find a checkerboard with some of the pieces still intact. I had never played but knew of those who did and I was quite excited by this new acquisition.

By the time we returned to Amos' mud-brick house, we had taken a few drinks from our stash and were feeling optimistic again.

"There is a small caravan forming south of Rimmon. I have heard from one of my fellow soldiers that he will also be joining the ranks of Jerubbaal and he wishes to come with us. There is safety in numbers so we shall travel with them. Do you have all your affairs in order?" Amos said with a serious tone born of suspicion.

"We do." I showed him all of what we intended to bring, not to mention the lack of water.

"I have some unleavened bread and some vegetables that I grew. That should provide us at the start and I trust that Yahweh will provide the rest." He bowed his head and began to pray over our journey once more. This prayer was shorter and the lightness in my head was grateful for that. We turned south and began our journey.

* * * * *

Our tiny caravan consisted of four men around my age, single and unknown to each other. I tried not to assume the worst, but there was a nagging feeling in the back of my head that they were on the run from something. They kept to themselves and spoke to no one. They did not seem to know each other and were content to leave it as such. There was an older man who I doubted could make it to our destination and I worried for his health. At his age, he should be resting on a farm somewhere with his children tending to his needs. There were two families. One family had two children, both female, and another family had three children, two boys, and one girl. They did not know each other as well, but the children rectified that within the first few miles of the journey. They bundled together and laughed and giggled at whispered utterances that did not concern the adults.

I nodded politely when eye contact was made but mostly stayed with Amos, Tabor, and Amos' friend, Yakov. Yakov was as sturdy as Amos and a little taller. He had brown curly hair that hung to his shoulders and a sharp nose that appeared to have been broken at some point in his life. A nasty scar ran from his right ear down to the corner of his mouth and he rubbed the area often. He barely spoke but assumed the leadership role of our caravan.

"The caravan ends at Shunem. For those who wish to fight against the Midianites, that is where your journey ends as well. For those who do not, it is but a short journey to Meggido. We can offer no protection after Shunem though."

Having said his piece, he turned and began to walk. Some glances were shared amongst the strangers but the conversation was held to a minimum. It felt wrong to begin such a grand journey in such a hushed tension, but that was the reality of the situation.

I don't know why, but once we were a distance away from Rimmon, I expected a dramatically different landscape to be witnessed. It was not. The same mixture of palm, olive, and oak trees dotted the horizon. The hills were densely overgrown, covered with a thick scrub of pine, oak, and terebinth trees. Terraced fields of grain lined the road from local farmers.

The monotony of the walk began to set in and my mind drifted to Padma. I feared for my emotional state so I engaged in the one trick that always delivered. I took the lid off my flask and took a long drink. This went on for a couple of hours and in the heat of the midday sun, I became lightheaded. I contemplated asking the caravan to take a break but I could not justify such things when the old man was still huffing along at a swift pace. If he could do it, I could.

When we approached a grove of olive trees, Yakov announced that we could take a short respite amidst the shade. I looked upward and said a silent prayer to the God that I was apparently serving now. I sat on the ground and wiped the sweat off my brow. Tabor sat next to me and Amos on the other side.

"This is the farthest I have ever been from home," I announced.

"Doesn't look much different than Rimmon. The route we are taking does not offer much in terms of variety." Amos said, drinking what I assumed was water.

"I can't see ever returning home," I said, surprising myself.

"No one knows what the future might hold," Tabor said ominously. He also took a drink and I honestly had no idea what was in his flask. He began to search around on the ground and picked up a few small rocks.

"What on earth are you doing?" Amos asked.

"Just gathering pieces for my new game." Tabor said with a glint in his eye. He pulled out the checkerboard we had plundered earlier in the day.

Amos raised his eyebrows in surprise. "That might be a fun way to unwind at the end of the day." I was somewhat shocked that Amos would indulge in frivolous games. I wondered if he knew the rules of the game.

Our short rest ended and we continued on our way. The path we walked was obvious in some areas, but hard to find in others and it was only then that I realized how much blind faith I had placed in our guide. Once I had made up my mind to go, I assumed I would be on my own, but now I was grateful to be with this group, despite actually knowing a few of them. We walked until the sun began to hover slightly over the horizon line. We found a place to camp on a small hill that was mostly cleared by fire from local farmers to eventually plant crops.

The majority of the day, I cycled between feeling shaky and really good due to the wine intake but once we sat for good, I drank more aggressively. I worried about how long my supply would last, but not enough for it to slow me down. Tabor got the board out and started to arrange the pieces. Amos became instantly agitated.

"That is not how you set up a proper game!" He finally snapped and started to arrange the pieces in an order I began to understand. The Individual group of men spread out and kept to themselves, obviously with no interest in making new acquaintances. Yakov sat near us but paid us no mind and the families rested together in a larger group. The old man seemed out of sorts and eventually settled near us, his curiosity peaked at the thought of gameplay.

Amos explained the rules of the game to us, but my wine-soaked brain had trouble following so I ended up just sitting there, nodding as if I understood. Every time Tabor went to make a move, Amos would snap, "No! You can't do that." and Tabor would just smile. This, of course, irritated Amos even more.

Eventually, Amos grew so exasperated that the old man finally intervened.

"May I give it a go?"

Amos threw his hands up in the air and replied, "By all means. You try teaching the imbecile. He couldn't learn how to operate a stick."

Tabor's grin grew even bigger as the old man took Amos' place. I realized that I had finally had too much and I lay on my blanket with my eyes closed in the hopes that no one had noticed how drunk I really was. I listened to the rhythmic, patient voice of the old man as he explained the rules. My thoughts drifted toward memories of my father. In the rare moments of lucidity, he had treated me with patience and kindness. I realized just then how much I missed him. I missed my father from my younger years. He would have known exactly what to do. Maybe I wouldn't be wandering around, drunk in the wilderness, with no discernable path. Of course, the father of my later years would have been no actual help, but I would have at least been able to take comfort in the fact he was here.

Chapter 11

The next morning brought an immense aching in the back of my head with it. I had a sudden urge to vomit but remembered that I was surrounded by veritable strangers and desperately wanted to avoid that scene. I calmed myself by taking deep breaths and trying to push the sickness as deep down in my belly as I could. I found that I had to utilize this strategy far too often. If there was any doubt about how wretched I looked, it was eradicated when I saw how Amos looked at me as I rose. His eyes lingered somewhere between judgment and sympathy so I focused on packing my things up. I picked up the flask and tried to sneak a sip. I was far too emotionally crushed when I realized that it was empty.

I reached into my bag and tried to secretly pour more into it from the larger jug. Of course, there was no way to accomplish this discreetly.

"I will be happy when your supply is exhausted." Amos said, somewhere behind me.

I had a flash of panic at his recognition, but it was quickly replaced by shame.

"It will be soon enough," I said, resigning to the fact he knew. I might as well take the drink if I no longer had to hide it. Amos said nothing more, he just kicked Tabor to wake him up and started packing up his own things.

"We will leave in five minutes. Everyone, prepare yourselves and we will continue on." Yakov bellowed with one hand resting on an olive tree.

I fought the urge to vomit once more when I stood. I realized that I had not eaten any actual food the day before and vowed to correct that today. I just hoped I could keep it down. We began walking and fell into the same pattern as the day before. I knew that my supply would probably only last one more day. Maybe it was for the best. If I was going to stop drinking, this trip would be as good a time as any.

I finally decided to break the silence and verify that Amos was not upset with me.

"What shall we expect when we get there?"

Amos, maintaining eye contact with the skyline before us, said "I can only go by my experiences with Deborah. At first, they will try to organize the soldiers into a presentable army."

"Am I presentable?" Tabor said, half-smiling.

"Fortunately for you, they will accept anyone. Most of the people who show up, in fact, are just like you. Most will not even have weapons to fight with. There are few you have slings, spears, knives, swords, shovels. Basically, if it can kill a man, they will have it."

I was thankful that I at least had a knife. The idea of engaging in a battle with my bare hands was not a notion I was favorable to.

"They will divide the army and go over basic strategy. The hope is that we outnumber the Midianites by so much, they choose not to fight at all. From the messages that I have received, that is a strong possibility. Sentiment has grown like wildfire at the resentment of the impoverished state that we have been reduced to."

"I admit, with shame in my heart, I have a great amount of fear." I said.

"God is with us. He will use our powerful numbers to overcome our oppressors. Your fear is unfounded and only hinders what you will be able to accomplish. Having said that, I truly understand. Once, I had fear in my heart as well. It passes." Amos said as he turned to look at me in the hopes of offering a source of optimism.

"The only victory that I am certain of," Tabor interjected, "is my inevitable victory against you, Amos. I will dominate you in checkers this evening when we make camp."

"You think I am going to attempt to play again with someone who is equipped with the mental capacity of a small child?" irritation began to reside in his features once more.

"You are scared. That is understandable. You have no chance against my newfound strategies." Tabor said with a straight face. I couldn't help but notice the old man, walking slightly ahead of us, begin to smile.

Amos grunted and we continued on in silence again. The wine began to take effect after we walked for a period and I told myself to be more careful today. I would need to save some for the morning. If I was feeling particularly strong, I would try to save some for when we actually got to the gathering of soldiers. Perhaps, wine would be offered to us there. I doubted this since it was such a righteous endeavor, but I could hold out hope.

We made camp a little earlier than the previous day because we found a nice hill by a river. I decided that I would try to introduce water to my diet. This seemed to refresh me and I was able to stay more clear-headed. When Tabor broke out the checkerboard again, Amos rolled his eyes. I was able to be more present and I sat next to the old man to watch the epic struggle commence.

"Do you think you were more effective in teaching our young friend than Amos there?" I asked the old man. Amos gave me a vicious glance and Tabor just smiled.

"I found him to be an inquisitive student of the game. I think he will do just fine."

The pieces moved all around the board and Amos began to get frustrated again. Only this time, it was because he was losing pieces at a rapid pace. I began to understand how the game was played but was not able to derive any real strategy as to how to go about it yet. A short time passed before Tabor made his final move and defeated Amos.

Amos' mouth dropped open as he stared at the board. "How did you..?"

Tabor just grinned as he reset the pieces, "Do not lose heart, Amos. I will teach you how to play this game if you wish."

Amos turned his attention to the old man. "I tried to teach him long after the sunset yesterday and he could barely grip the pieces. You play a game or two and now he is a champion?"

The old man smiled and replied, "The wise in heart shall be called prudent: And the sweetness of the lips increaseth learning; Proverbs 16:21. You have leadership potential in you but with a harsh tone, you do not invite questioning. A leader is also a teacher. Kindness is a much better educator than fear. The Lord sometimes uses sharp rebukes to teach a lesson. They teach because they instill a pain in us that we don't ever want to repeat. Sometimes the Lord teaches us with kindness. For encouragement offers blessings beyond measure. Both of these types of corrections are always made with love. That means everything. Anything in between is a waste of breath. It is a lazy attempt at controlling someone else's actions to adhere to our own expectations. "

The rebuke was sharp, but it was delivered with such pleasantry, Amos could only smile. "Message received." was all he could reply as he began to reset his own pieces.

"So you are a man who knows the Hebrew texts?" I asked, surprised. I didn't believe that I knew anyone who could read, much less was experienced in the Holy writings.

"I was blessed to have been exposed and taught some readings." the old man humbly replied.

"You must know everything there is to know about Yahweh." I made the overly simplistic statement and immediately cursed myself for sounding like a child.

"Knowing the text and knowing our Heavenly Father are two different things. I have met many who have read the text and believed to know all there is to know. That is not the way of our Lord. Men with no questions to ask are to be feared for they are filled with arrogance and false bravado. Avoid them at all costs and always have an inquisitive nature about you."

I nodded. I barely understood anything he said, but was able to assemble some summary of it in my own understanding. I had an abundance of questions but did not even have the ability to form them into proper words. I drank more and turned my attention toward their next game. Tabor won again and I had built up enough courage to try a game for myself.

Where Tabor had to labor to win games against Amos, he made quick work of me. I just laughed when the game ended abruptly and all of my pieces resided on Tabor's side of the board. We fell into easy conversation after the game and eventually, we lay on our own blankets and fell asleep.

The following day was when my wine supply dried up. Depression and anxiety flooded my very being so I tried to simply focus on each and every minute detail of our journey. I took one step at a time as the wine wore off. I knew what would come next. Soon, nausea and tremors would overcome me. The rest of the trip would be spent in sober misery.

Chapter 12

Yakov announced in the morning that our journey to Shunem would conclude on this very day. I started my day by vomiting everything I had consumed the day prior. Of course, this was only a couple of figs and a lot of water, but it came out with fury. Tabor and Amos were kind enough not to say anything. I debated asking Tabor if he had managed to sustain his wine supply but didn't want to draw more attention to myself.

We crested a hill and I was not prepared for the vision that I would see. On the plains below us stood more people than I previously thought existed on the earth. I was paralyzed by shock and the obsessions of my mind were temporarily halted.

"These people are all here to fight for Jerubbaal?" The words escaped my mouth in a barely audible whisper.

Amos smiled grandly and said, "I believe they are." He turned and put his hands on my shoulders in elation, "As I said, fear is unnecessary. With a force of this size, we can not be defeated." He laughed as he turned to the crowd once more. The families and the men who did not wish to fight were given directions around the opulent gathering of men. They departed our company without a word. The only ones left standing on the hill were the old man, Yakov, Amos, Tabor, and I.

"You will be joining the fray?" I asked the old man incredulously.

"I'm not much of a fighter but I have some wisdom to impart. I'll contribute however I can." He said in what I believed to be a noble understatement.

"Let us discover our destiny, men!" Amos said with a slap on the back. I was jarred forward and nearly stumbled from the impact but shared his enthusiasm. As we descended the hill towards the mass gathering, I noticed plumes of smoke from the various fires that people gathered around. Tents, too many to count, were spread around the plains. Camels, donkeys, and goats all dotted the landscape. A platform had been constructed on the North side of the crowd and I surmised that that was where the leadership to this endeavor would be found.

"Let us head to the stage and see what the procedure for involvement entails." Amos said, obviously making the same assumption that I had.

As we made our way north, I took stock of the men that I would be accompanying into battle. Some looked the part of a warrior. One man stood nearly a foot taller than me, and I had considered myself fairly tall. Others were much shorter than me and so thin that it looked like a breeze could topple them. I judged each and every man I saw, going back and forth about feeling better about my chances to feeling as if I had no chance at all at survival. Amos had been correct regarding the weapons as well. Many men were empty-handed but I saw everything from an ox goad to a sling. Various states of armor were also donned, though most had nothing more than a linen tunic.

The noise was deafening. Most men were talking over one another enthusiastically. The energy of the crowd was evident. Others rested in isolation, ruminating in fear, anxiety, or impatience at inactivity. I overheard snippets of conversation as we passed through.

"...I hear they have chariots made of iron..."

"...We will outnumber them ten to one..."

"...My farm was reduced to ashes..."

The phrases floated in and around my head. I wanted to hear more from each conversation being held, but we were moving at a brisk pace. Some things I heard I could relate to. Some things I heard worried me. I had never seen iron, only heard that it was much stronger than any of the metals that I had ever encountered. I liked the idea of outnumbering our enemy ten to one if that were true.

I made sure to stay close, directly behind Amos, and could feel that Tabor had grabbed my tunic so that we would not be separated. When we finally reached the platform, Yakov and the old man were nowhere to be seen. I felt a sense of sadness at their disappearance and wondered if I would ever see them again.

We approached the platform where a group of armored soldiers, obviously battle-tested veterans, stood with their backs to us.

"Excuse me. May I have a word?" Amos bellowed with authority. One of the soldiers turned around at my friend's voice that rose above the roar of the crowd. He had a sword tied to his side and his armor shone in the sunlight. He walked over with no real expression on his face.

"What do you need?" He said as he bent down to get closer to Amos' face.

"What do we need to do to fight alongside Jerubbaal?" Amos yelled, despite the intimate proximity to the soldiers.

"As of now, nothing is to be done but wait. We will have orders to deliver shortly. Just stay vigilant and patient." The soldier turned and walked back to the group. I looked closer at the group and saw a man who enigmatically stood out from the others who surrounded him. He looked like a soldier but the military personnel around him regarded him as a king.

I studied his face to see if I could discern what made this man seem above all the others. He was talking to his core group of soldiers around him, but I could not make out his words. It was obvious that he spoke with passion, conviction, and intelligence. He had curly, light brown hair that was cut short and a full beard.

"That is him. That is Jerubbaal." I said in Amos' ear.

Amos followed my eyes and replied, "I have no proof of that, but I believe you are right. Let us separate from this crowd." He said as he inched to the side. Once out of the center of the masses, we were able to speak at normal volume again.

"I get the feeling we will not be here long. It would not surprise me if we were on the move again before the day ends." Amos said.

"After the effort to get here, my legs could use a little rest." Tabor said with a hint of irritation in his voice.

"Battle requires far more exertion. Allow the strength you have gained to fuel you for what comes next." Amos said, unconcerned with Tabor's physical state.

"Always comforting, Amos. You are like a soft, warm blanket." Tabor replied sarcastically.

Amos rolled his eyes and sat on the ground and waited. The sun traveled far across the sky before anything developed. A great roar from the crowd erupted and we all stood and turned toward the platform. The man we believed to be Jerubbaal walked towards the front of the make-shift stage. He stood with great authority and waited for the noise to alleviate.

I believed there was no way imaginable that this raucous group of men would ever close their mouths long enough to hear a sentence that this man would utter, but sure enough, within moments, all we could hear was the breeze that rustled our hair.

"I am Gideon, also known as Jerubbaal." He had intended to say more but the crowd let loose another round of cheers that shook the stage he stood upon. He lifted his right hand and the crowd was instantly silenced again. "I am honored to stand before such righteous men as yourselves."

The man was entrancing. I hung on him every word and any doubt about my current situation was erased by this man's presence.

"As Israelites, we are all brothers in our Creator. I am equal and no better than any of you. I am a simple man from the tribe of Manasseh. I did not wish for any of this. I am compelled to act only due to the fact that our Father in Heaven has called me to once and for all, deliver us from the outsiders that now plague our land. I was threshing wheat on my farm when he spoke to me. He told me to gather an army and he would deliver us from our oppressors."

Another round of guttural screams interrupted him again. He seemed undeterred.

"Many say that we are an unbeatable army due to our size. We are, in fact, a formidable force to be sure but the notion that we are larger than the Midianites is completely false. My scouts tell me that the Midianite army numbers close to 135,000. This same Midianite army that has cursed us with death and poverty is close by. They have taken everything from us with superior numbers and superior armament. Make no mistake, though. We are undefeatable because the Lord has made a promise that we will be victorious!"

I had been mesmerized and recharged by each word he spoke until he revealed the discrepancy in our numbers. I had placed all of my hopes and optimism into the belief that we would simply stand before them as they retreated without a fight. To hear that they outnumbered us deflated any confidence that I had. Throw in the fact that they were infinitely more armored than us, which was equally disheartening. I had the sudden urge to turn around and leave. The only thing that stopped me was knowing that there was nowhere to go.

"I have aroused the anger of the invaders by destroying the idols that they worship. They gather in large numbers and know of our imminent aggression. They do not know where it will come from, nor when it will take place. They only know it is coming. Have heart, though! We will be under the banner of protection from our Lord and Creator!"

If anyone else was as nervous as I was, they did a fantastic job of hiding it for another hearty cheer rose from the group.

"Rest now, for when night falls, we will begin our movement. Stay vigilant! Pray for protection and courage. We will have our place in history before all is said and done." He turned and left to much applause. The crowd dispersed and meandered back to their campfires and small groups.

"He is quite the speaker." Tabor said when the three of them found a place to settle until the movement started.

"That is what I have heard." Amos responded, "and now I know it is true. He is obviously a man who has communicated with the Lord. We are in good hands despite the odds being stacked against us."

I must have looked nervous because Amos patted me on the back.

"You comfort him, but not me." Tabor declared with a mock look of indignation.

"Be careful, Tabor. I may start to actually consider you a friend. Neither one of us needs that."

"I will do my best to repulse you in the future."

"I do not doubt it."

"I'm not sure we are doing the right thing." The words sounded so cowardly as they exited my mouth. I regretted the statement but could not hide the sentiment.

"You must have faith. Believe that there is a power above us and he cares for us and will keep us safe."

"I have seen how he protects his people!" I shot back. "I saw one of his '*protected*' underneath the rubble of the only house I had ever known. I am no better than my father. I should have the same fate as him."

Fury and indecision muddled my mind and it also probably didn't help that I was still reeling from the lack of wine.

"I need to take a walk." I angrily spat as I stood up. I had made up my mind to find someone, anyone, who shared my aversion to sobriety. I determined that the best way to find the cure for my craving would be to find a rough-looking, raucous crowd. If anyone could identify men who would frequent wine shops, it was me.

I walked far into the crowd so that Tabor and Amos lost sight of me. I must have looked like I was stalking my prey, looming suspiciously in the background. A painful amount of time inched by and then I spied my target. A man who looked to be my age was pouring something from a large jug into a small flask and the purple hue was unmistakable. Now I had to calculate my approach.

"Hello, kind brethren. Might you be able to spare some of your beverage?" I said in my smoothest tone. The man looked at me with slight suspicion and I began to worry that I had ruined my opportunity. A slow smile started to spread across his face.

"Sure, friend. Always willing to help a thirsty brother." He tilted the jug up to fill my flask and relief permeated my body.

"Much appreciated, good man. Good luck in...battle." I gave an awkward wave and walked away, cringing at my choice of words. I must have looked like a complete fool. I comforted myself with the knowledge that I had my fill of wine. I gulped it fast for the full effect. This would have mortified any proper wine enthusiast, but I had a goal and it was to get there as expediently as possible. I kept my eyes peeled for another source as I slowly wandered around the camp. When my drink was almost completely gone, I found another group who were sharing their wine copiously so I gently forced my way into their circle. It worked like a charm.

On this trip of plunder, I was forced to interact more than I cared to. The conversation flowed and the gentlemen that I happened to be conversing with were of a more violent nature than I. I tried to imitate their bloodlust with my only intention of getting more wine. I managed to fill my flask once more, completely forgetting that we were to move out before the night fell.

I looked around to center myself by using the platform, but it had been completely dismantled. I was lost in the crowd and panic began to fill me. What was I going to do? The wine had convinced me that abandoning the cause was not a viable option, but I was not about to go through with this theater if I did not have Amos or Tabor to fight alongside me.

My heart beat faster and faster and my head began to spin. I tried to get outside the center of the crowd, the outskirts where fewer people were. I found a tree with no one around. I decided that I would make myself easier to find by sitting underneath it. I had no hope of finding my friends but I would make it as easy as possible for them to spot me. I sat and decided that I would close my eyes for just a moment. I was so tired. The emotional drain of the day combined with the wine that I had imbibed so quickly left me unable to maintain consciousness. As I drifted off, I let the panic dissipate and resolved that whatever happened would happen. I simply did not care anymore.

Chapter 13

The storm before the storm was so much more violent than I ever remember it being. I knew that I was awake and not dreaming, but could not force myself to open my eyes yet. My body was moving somehow. This had to be a dream. It was so loud. There were people around me, this much I knew. Eventually, I found the ability to open my eyes and I stared at the moving ground. My arms were both elevated. I realized that Amos and Tabor were laboriously carrying me forward amidst the massive parade of soldiers.

"I'm going to throw up." I said in a loud whisper.

"Wonderful!" Amos said in a voice dripping with indignation. "Over there."

Tabor shifted and we separated ourselves from the rest of the men. I kneeled by some brush on the side of the path and began to heave. The first three attempts produced nothing, but the fourth was a colossal success. I emptied my stomach and instantly felt better. I was sure that people were staring as they passed by and that notion of not caring about anything was replaced by deep, deep shame.

"I do not wish to spend my night watching you water this brush with your insides. We must keep moving." Amos grunted. His compassionate, reassuring self was now just fury and anger.

"I can..." I had no idea what I meant to say but it did not matter since another stream of vomit made its way to the ground. I did not see that one coming.

"I'm good. Let's go." I managed to stutter as I stood. I swayed back and forth a little as I stood by the brush and noticed streams of brown vomit streaking my tunic. I began to waddle forward in the same direction as the rest of the Israelites and avoided looking at either Tabor or Amos. I knew the conversation that was to come but was not eager to start it now.

"Where is his flask?" I heard Amos bark.

"I've emptied it and filled it with water." Tabor responded. They were talking about me like I wasn't here. Then I got irritated that they had wasted the wine that I had worked so hard to secure.

"I'm sure you emptied alright."

"I'm not the one who had to be carried for the last two hours." Tabor defended himself.

Guilt began to seep in. How humiliating it must have been to find me and have to drag me along in front of all these people. This only proved that I was not fit to be a soldier. They should have just left me under the tree and gone on their way. I would have gone back home, sold my land, and used the proceeds to finally drink myself to death in that cave outside Rimmon. Instead, I was still drunk and taking a long walk to my inevitable murder.

"I'm sorry." I said. The slurred words fell on deaf ears. They did not want to hear such pitiful offerings from me so I decided that I would speak no more. I simply focused on my feet and tried not to fall. I heard a couple of people laughing as they passed us and I could only assume I was the source of their amusement. The next time our roving band of marauders stopped, I would run away. I should not serve as an anchor to men who aspired to greater things. I had fallen for the lie that I could be used by God for greater glory.

I spent the next hour reliving all of my failures in my head to try and prove that I was useless to the kingdom of heaven, justifying my impending escape.

"So what did you learn on your little scouting mission?" Tabor said to Amos. I, of course, was completely unaware of what any of this meant.

"It was actually very informative, thank you." Amos said with great agitation. "I talked to Gideon himself. I think he was quite impressed with me."

"Who wouldn't be?" Tabor replied sarcastically. Amos ignored this and continued.

"I told him of my service to Deborah and he said that I would be of great value to him. He also informed me that the Midianites have formed an alliance with the men of Amalek and some other tribes from the east. There are too many to count. They have crossed the Jordan River in what he suspects is a precursor to the attempted slaughter of the Israelites."

"That is hardly good news." Tabor interrupted.

"Only if you believe that God is not with us. Gideon destroyed a monument of Ba'al and replaced it with an altar for Yahweh and this has unified many different peoples against us. He is a brave man."

"I'd call him reckless."

"I find it comical that you would call anyone reckless. He is a man with great faith and passion. This does not always coalesce with the way of the world. It should be honored and respected. It only solidifies my conviction to serve him however I can. I challenge you to adopt this view."

"I have thrown my lot in. I am fully committed to this tragic course and do not wish for a way out. It is just a little bit more than daunting to consider that at the beginning of the day we were told that our forces outnumbered any on earth, and now we hear that we pale in comparison to this great eastern threat."

"Numbers do not matter to the Almighty. To show his strength and glory, He will use the exact number that he sees fit. I am just proud to be amongst them."

"They have iron weaponry. They have chariots! Have you ever seen a chariot? I know that I have not. I know only that they are too fast for a man on foot and can disembowel a person before they even know they have sustained a wound. This does not sound like a divine fight to me."

"What would you know of the divine?"

"I assume it means to keep your bowels intact."

"God will provide."

"That is your grand military strategy? God will provide? No wonder I beat you at checkers. I am tired of this topic. I no longer wish to meditate on the might of our enemy."

"That is fine by me."

I would say that silence ensued after that declaration but the marching of thousands of men in the night was anything but reticent. They had at least come to a mutual agreement to cease talking. This was fine by me. I had started to sober up a bit due to the exertion but nausea and the shakes had returned. I finally felt that I had regained my wits and could join my companions in the present. I made conscientious efforts to walk more upright and with confidence.

By the time we stopped for the night, near morning, my physical misery was in full swing. Had I not learned to forecast these consequences before hoisting the flask to my lips? The path we traveled was wide, but we opted to find an incline and made camp in an elevated status.

I broke my hours-long vow of silence to say, "I apologize for my indiscretion. You can rest assured that no repeat of the incident will occur."

"Amos and Tabor both stared at the ground. Tabor finally responded, "Apology accepted. I will admit anger at the indignity of having to carry you for so long but I am in no position to judge."

Amos added, "You are one of my oldest friends, Ethan, but I can not fathom your cravings for such behavior. I accept your apology. I can only pray that you find a way to avoid such pitfalls in the future."

"Thank you both. It has become obvious to me that I can't continue down this path. You both should see by now that I am not fit to serve Gideon. I am a liability that is not needed in battle, especially a battle that looms against so many odds."

More silence followed. Amos thoughtfully said, "If that is the decision that you have come to in your mind, I only ask that you tell

Gideon himself. You have made it this far and I believe he deserves an explanation as to how you have come to this conclusion."

My first reaction was to blurt out 'absolutely not'. I had been subject to enough humiliation already, I was not about to present myself to potentially the greatest man I would ever meet and explain to him that I was too cowardly to proceed. My hesitation brought a little more reason and clarity, though, so I finally said, "I will then."

"Since you have made up your mind, I see no point in waiting. Now is as good a time as any. I will come with you."

"As will I." Tabor chimed in.

"Do you not trust me to do this on my own? I have cost you much exhaustion this day. You deserve to finally rest and rejuvenate. This is something I should do on my own." I said, still harboring hope that I may sneak away without detection.

"I do trust you, I only wish to offer you support. After all, it is the sole reason that I am here." Amos said as he stood once more.

"Let's get to it then." Tabor said, dramatically rising, emphasizing his distaste for more physical movement.

"So be it." I said as I stood last. If I could endure fifteen more minutes of embarrassment, I would be free of all of this obligation and misery. Such a failed endeavor I had never embarked upon.

Chapter 14

The ground was wet with morning dew as we passed the multitude of soldiers that separated us from Gideon. I fought back the shame as I passed people who must have witnessed my behavior in my lowest moments. My stomach clenched in agony at the thought of what I was about to do. I cursed myself for wishing I had some wine to steady my nerves. The wondrous cycle continues without end.

As Tabor, Amos, and I approached Gideon's tent, he was stretching his fleece out, flat on a rock. He looked like he had the weight of the world on his shoulders but stared intently at the task at hand. The way his eyes shone in the dawn that streamed through the surrounding olive trees displayed why these men traveled great distances to serve him. They held integrity and intensity that inspired jealousy within me. I wanted to be like him.

This realization only made my forthcoming words more excruciating. He looked up and saw us approaching and stood with the grace of a gazelle.

"Amos!" he cheered in greeting. "It is Amos, correct?"

Amos smiled at the impressive memory of this man. How many strangers had he met recently? "That is correct. I do not wish to bother you..."

Gideon waved the notion away. I couldn't help but notice the animation of each expression.

"It is no bother at all. Welcome. How can I be of service?"

He stood facing us, fully present with his company. His entire world seemed to halt with each interaction he had, placing full attention on the man in front of him.

"I just wanted you to meet my friends that I told you about. This is Ethan and Tabor of Rimmon, from the tribe of Zebulun." Amos directed his attention our way and I immediately felt like retreating within myself.

Gideon stepped forward and looked me in the eyes with a full, genuine smile. "Amos has told me all about you. It is a pleasure to meet you Ethan, and Tabor. Peace be unto you." My knees began to buckle as he embraced me and kissed me on the cheek. He moved on to Tabor while I wondered what Amos had told him.

Amos interjected, "Ethan has something that he would like to say. It was a pleasure to see you again, Gideon."

"You as well." Gideon turned his full attention towards me and I wiped the sweat from my brow as I broke eye contact with him and looked off into the distance. I fumbled with my hands, unsure of how to even stand before this man.

"I...I don't really know where to start." I stammered.

"Relax. You are amongst family here. There is no need to worry. How can I help you?"

"I appreciate what you are trying to do. The Midianites are a plague upon our land and our people. The bravery that you are demonstrating and your faith in Yahweh are admirable." I knew that I was only biding time, trying to talk my way out of responsibilities with complimentary rhetoric, but I did believe the words I spoke. "I regret to say that I am not worthy of such a noble endeavor. I must return home." The words were out now. It was almost over. There were so many people here, surely he would grant me this one allowance. What would one less soldier mean to this force that had flocked to serve him?

"Why do you feel that you are not worthy to fight alongside these men?" He looked honestly confused at my assertion.

"I have seen those around me. They are fit and proper soldiers. They are of good, moral character. They feel passion and certainty in the cause that you fight for. I am riddled with self-doubt and fear. It is hard enough to request leave, all that I ask of you is that you do not make me go through the litany of reasons I am not fit to serve you." I was now begging and it sounded so pathetic and shameful.

Gideon stepped closer and I worried that he would be able to smell the wine through my very pores. "Young man, I am sorry to say that I do not believe you. I mean no disrespect, mind you." He put his hands on my shoulder in a shocking display of familiarity. "I believe that you are here, right where you are supposed to be. You belong on this plot of land as much as any individual that surrounds us, including me."

I felt a lump form in my throat. The last thing I needed right now was to cry in front of this man. That would be the greatest shame to endure above all else. "But...but you do not know what I have done." *and please don't make me tell you.*

Gideon smiled. He smiled! "I know. Isn't that wonderful? That's the most glorious component of this entire venture. None of us here knows what anyone else has done. We are all immaculate strangers gathered under the banner of a great cause. Your past does not matter. To call yourself inferior for days that have passed is an unnecessary exercise. Do you know where I was when I was called to serve?"

I shook my head but was most assured that it was not at a pagan temple, inebriated beyond recognition.

"I was threshing wheat, cowering in a shed trying to hide from the Midianites. I was the least of my family in the least important tribe of Israel. I was simply known as Joash's son, nothing more. I had never raised a weapon against anyone in my life. I was inferior in every manner possible. But, I was still called to serve our Creator!"

"I do not wish to go into detail, but I have done far worse than cower in fear and hide from the enemy."

"Then you serve as the perfect weapon against our enemy. If the least of these can defeat those that defile His name, what does that say for our heavenly father?" His voice grew quieter but more impassioned. "We were all mired in the secrecy of our own personal sin. Alone in a world of death, cruelty, and chaos. He called us together to be his body. We were not destined for this solitude you wish to return to. Amidst all this..." he waved his hand in a grand gesture to the masses that wandered all around us. "You stand here, the most important cog in this grand machine. You, Ethan! I see within you a purpose you are completely unaware of. That is why you are surrounded by people who see it when you can't. Of course, you are free to go, but think about what you would be returning to." He pointed to the ground on which I stood and with a powerful voice added, "This! This is right where you are supposed to be. Do you know what I did when I heard the voice of the almighty calling me to action?"

"Yahweh talked directly to you?" I questioned, ignoring his original query.

"He did. It was overwhelming. It filled me with fear and purpose all at once. What does one do when they hear the voice of God, Himself? They follow blindly, right?"

I nodded, unsure. I had never been blessed with such a message. I wanted to simply deny that this had ever happened but the manner in which he spoke shouted that it was all true.

"No. I questioned Him. I doubted Him. I blamed him for handing his people over to the Midianites! I put Him to the test. I brought an offering before him to see if it truly was Yahweh. I put the tip of my staff to the offering and it was immediately consumed by fire. I destroyed an altar of Ba'al and immediately constructed one for Yahweh. That was still not enough for me. I put him to the test once more. I asked him to make my fleece..." He ran over and picked the fleece up that he had placed on the rock while we approached and brought it back to us, "This fleece. I placed it on the threshing floor and asked him to make it wet with dew while the ground remained desert dry. The next morning, it was so. This was still not enough. I was filled with doubt and inferiority, just like you and I asked that it be completely dry the next day while the earth was dampened, and it was so. It took me a while but I finally listened to the calling in which I received. We all move at different paces and hide in unique locations, but He finds us nonetheless. The most important act we can perform is to listen when He does."

He placed the fleece down just as he had before and returned to me. "Ethan, as I said. You are free to go. All I ask is that you try to pray and determine if that is the course which you truly should embark upon." Once again, he placed his hands on my shoulders and squeezed them.

I nodded and attempted a smile. "Thank you, Gideon." I shuddered at the thought I had just called him by name, but he smiled in reassurance. He released me and I turned to go.

"It was an honor to have met you, Ethan." I turned and nodded again. I walked towards Amos and Tabor, not realizing they had not meandered too far off. They said nothing as I joined their ranks and we walked slowly back to where we had made camp for the evening.

It took a few seconds before I realized that Tabor had tears in his eyes. He must have heard the entire conversation and it struck a nerve in his heart. I had been intent on returning to my land but now I was left more confused than ever. It only took a few moments in time, but now I was certain that this was where I was supposed to be. I would stay for a couple more days and see what happens. That was how I came to grips with my situation. I didn't make a long-term commitment, a declaration of a lifestyle change. I just reasoned I would stay for a couple more days. That seemed easy enough.

Amos and Tabor both used their intuition in dealing with the unfolding events and neither said anything. They knew that I was deep in thought and conversation would only be a hindrance to what needed to be done next. I lay on my blanket, feeling the cooling air soothe my nerves. The shakes and nausea had gone. The desire to seek out and find a wineskin had passed. The uncertain future brought peace instead of angst through this evening.

Chapter 15

In my experience, moments of great inspiration come with quick expiration dates. The feeling of driving purpose that I experienced walking away from Gideon that day was fleeting. We began to march the next day to an unknown destination. Once again, doubt and fear crept in, but I found the resolve to fulfill my obligation. I found comfort in Amos and Tabor who found common ground in looking after me. I longed to be near Gideon again though, as it steeled my will.

He would often make appearances along the line to girder morale, but they seemed too few and far in between to offer me any sustained confidence. For the first time along that walk, I used the spare moments of silence to attempt to pray. I had picked up from Amos, to begin with, 'Dear Heavenly Father....' I don't know if this was how everyone prayed, but I found it convenient to have a prompt to help me begin. I asked for peace in my soul. I had no idea what that would even feel like amidst all the hostility that reigned supreme within me, but I needed it so desperately. I prayed for our safe return and I prayed that I represented him with honor.

It occurred to me somewhere on day three of our seemingly endless walk, that I had not prayed for victory over the Midianites. I don't know if this was my subconscious way of avoiding thinking about the inevitable confrontation but I found that it eased my mind just a bit to allow me to function.

"I'm glad you chose to stay with us." Amos finally said after a prolonged silence. He did not look directly at me, just straight ahead. Always, straight ahead. He was as filthy as the rest of us from the dust and dirt of the roads but appeared somehow stronger than when we first set out. He was built for this type of life. I was bordering on exhaustion and did not know how to respond.

"Thank you for the kind sentiments." This seemed to come across as disingenuous, but it was all that I could offer at the moment. I was sweating profusely and it felt like I hadn't stopped since we started our march.

"It is nice to have friends to walk with. I have often wondered how strong my passions would be for this mission, were it not for the two of you." Tabor said in an uncharacteristic moment of vulnerability.

"I am certain that I would not be here." I said truthfully. I would have been back home by now trying to scrape up enough shekels to buy my next round of drinks. The urge to imbibe came and went. The supply seemed to have run out so I had no options regardless. This was probably for the best for if the temptation were there, I don't believe I would have been able to resist it.

Finally, we stopped at the spring of Harod in the valley south of the hill of Moreh. It was a beautiful valley that offered spectacular views of the surrounding landscape. It was too beautiful for the mission we were on. I did not feel as if I deserved such respite, but when we stopped, I drank my body weight of water and found slumber quite easily.

The slumber offered no reprieve from the dreams of Padma and my father though. I would often end up in her arms again. In her embrace, I found joy that I had not known in reality. I stared at her face in an attempt to memorize each and every detail of her visage. I was cognizant that I was dreaming but tried to fully indulge at the moment nonetheless. She smiled at me and told me how proud she was of me.

"I haven't had a drink in three days," I said in my dream, stroking her hair like I used to do in the predawn moments, as the weak rays of the sun danced in her eyes.

"I know. You are doing so well." She would say as she gently kissed my forehead. I felt self-conscious, knowing how filthy I was, but remembered that it was my dream and I could be pure and pristine at this moment if I focused. "You need to see it through. Promise me?"

Any irritation I felt at constantly being reminded of the perilous situation I was in was quickly diminished by her touch. "I will. I promise." I said quietly.

"For me?" She said, pleading.

"For you." The dream always ended with me returning her kiss. I would wake up with a hole in my chest. I curled up on my blanket physically attempting to hold the pain at bay. I missed her more than I could express and lay there with tears streaming down my face in the dark. My congestion from the tears seemed thunderous in the silence. I was sure that Amos and Tabor were aware of my tears but once again, they said nothing to put the spotlight on my despair. I began to wonder what the point of this whole expedition was. Even if we were victorious; even if I was to remain home amongst the victors, she would not be there to greet me. What was the point if she was not there in the end?

My moments of bravery would come in the daylight, so I gave in to the loneliness under the cover of night. My thoughts turned to my father. It was well documented that he gave no credence to our people's plight, our history, but he still would have been proud that I was doing something...*anything*. I tried to picture him younger when he had life and energy within him. It was hard to do. I knew that he had been quite handsome in his youth. I bet he was charismatic and would have enjoyed this platform to perform. Of course, that was long ago. The shell of my father dominated the images in my head, though. I resented him for making this the case. When the sun rose, I wiped my tears away and sat up.

Amos had already awakened and was drinking water from his jug. The ground was wet and the heat from the day had not arrived yet to warm us. It was difficult to unwrap from the warmth of the blanket, but I did. There was no shaking, nausea, or headaches to hold me down now.

"What do you think will happen next?" I asked Amos, wiping the sleep from my eyes.

"I heard riders come in the middle of the night. I imagine they were scouts giving Gideon information about our enemy. My guess is that we should know soon." Tabor kept sleeping soundly, his snores providing the entertainment as we slowly nibbled on some figs that had been scavenged the day before. I had been hungry for three days and knew that they would not fill me up but knew that our next meal was never guaranteed.

"Does he always sleep so soundly?" Amos said, throwing pebbles at his head to try and rouse him.

"For as long as I have known him. Without a conscience, one finds sleep easy I surmise." I said, only half in jest. I had seen how much the raid of the Midianites had changed him. He still harbored some of his boyish nature about him, but he had also developed a somber tone to him. He had matured in a way that I don't believe I had. My father said I was born morose. Those with a poet's heart always are. I would think to myself, what a useless personality trait to one who doesn't have knowledge of the written language. My so-called 'poet's heart' was wasted on a drunk illiterate.

As the sun climbed higher in the sky, trumpets blared off in the distance and I jumped at the sound. Tabor slowly opened his eyes and sat up. He looked around at the pile of pebbles surrounding his head and looked at Amos.

"That is very mature - a grown man disturbing the earth for his own amusement." Tabor said, shaking his head taking no real offense.

"The pebble cares not where it lies." Amos responded as he stood and stretched in the face of the new day.

Gideon had climbed the hill with a few soldiers behind him and turned to face the crowd. I took notice that the old man who had taught Tabor checkers was one of those who stood behind him. He didn't speak a word, but he appeared to have a position of some importance. Tabor and I stood and we all walked over to where Gideon was. The crowd became dense and the cool morning air was warmed by the proximity of all the men who had gathered in this confined space to hear what Gideon had to say.

"Good morning, sons of Israel. Welcome to the day that is ours!" He was as animated as ever, even in this early morning hour. He seemed to exude a perpetual enthusiasm that once again sparked jealousy deep down in my stomach. The crowd did not reciprocate the energy and simply stood to hear what message was to be delivered.

"I have news to give unto you." I noticed that he did not classify the news as good or bad, it was just news. I guess he was leaving it up to us to assess.

"I have learned valuable information regarding our opponent. They have been spotted north of this hill, preparing for battle like we have. Our scouts have informed me that the rumors that we had heard are indeed true. The people of Midian have joined forces with the Amalek and others from the east." Gideon bellowed. My instinct sent me down a hole of frenzied thought. This was not good. The Midianites were a formidable army on their own. The fact that they felt compelled to join forces with their enemies against us, only reassured me they were bent on our annihilation.

"When we started out on this journey, we were resolute and determined to reach our objective. Nothing we have learned should change that now. Yes. We are outnumbered. The hope of overwhelming our opponents with our sheer size doesn't seem to be an option now, but that does not change the ferocity in which we will fight." He ran his fingers through his hair in a rare moment that displayed hesitancy.

"You know what we are up against. You know that they have more men than we do. You know that they have more weapons and armor than we do. You know that they are nearby and that our engagement is close at hand. Having been fully informed of the situation, I now say this to you." Gideon took another deep breath and ran both of his hands through his hair again. He seemed uncertain and turned from the crowd. The old man who we had traveled with, gave him a nod and Gideon turned back around. There was an absurdly long silence before Gideon spoke again.

"If any of you are timid or afraid, you may leave this mountain now and return to your homes." As he said this, Gideon's eyes found mine. My face turned flush and I couldn't look away. I was no great military scholar, but I had never heard of a leader, on the eve of battle, tell his men that they were free to leave if they harbored any fear within them! We were already outnumbered! Why had this invitation to desert us even been stated out loud? I could leave. I wanted the excuse, the opportunity to flee, and now I had it. If only Gideon had not looked at me. I cursed myself for being so hypnotized by this man I had just met.

Every muscle in my body urged me to turn and begin the shameful act of slinking away from the front, but I just stood. Murmurs rippled throughout the crowd. After a few long moments, someone near me turned and dropped their hoe on the ground. I looked as he walked back through the crowd. His shoulders were hunched, eyes staring at the ground trying to avoid judgment. A few more moments passed and one by one, others started to turn and leave as well. The man next to Amos said, "I can live with the Midianites' occasional raid. I'm not interested in a death sentence."

"What are you doing?" Amos said through gritted teeth. "Have some pride!"

"I'd rather have a home to return to." the man continued to walk away. Amos grabbed him by the shoulder but the man shook him off and continued on.

"We are proud Israelites! Do not abandon your brothers." Amos said in near panic as more people followed suit and began to walk back in the direction in which we had marched.

"I don't know you. You are not my brother." another voice rose above the crowd. At first, it was simply a few people who had begun to retreat, but the number got larger and larger. Some threw their weapons on the ground and made for a quick exit, others plundered what they could in what I assumed would be used to trade and barter for goods back home, never explaining the cowardly background of the acquisition of such goods.

I finally broke my gaze from Gideon and looked around. The whole crowd seemed to undulate as more and more broke through as if marching toward their exile. This was as disastrous an event as I thought possible. With the enemy so close, Gideon had just given permission for what looked like thousands of men to simply "change their mind" and walk back home. What was the reason for coming in the first place?

I immediately was hit with the hypocrisy of my own critical judgment. The only reason I was still transfixed in the spot where I stood is that I was too cowardly to move. My stomach twisted in knots as I watched more and more stream toward the well-worn road. I shifted my feet uncomfortably and both Tabor and Amos whipped their heads around to face me. My face, still burning red, avoided eye contact and I didn't move another inch.

How could they blame me now for leaving? By my limited estimation, over half of the army that set out to rid our lands of the people from the east were now marching back to serve them once more. Over half! I started rapidly looking back and forth between Gideon and the increasingly large exodus of retreating men.

What was going to happen next? Was Gideon going to stop them? That didn't seem to reconcile with his nature. Was he going to call off the entire battle? That also didn't seem like a likely outcome. Anyone who had talked to him for more than a moment could see and hear the determination in his eyes and voice.

"What do we do?" I asked Tabor in a labored, frenzied voice. Doubt started to crack through his confident facade. He pursed his lips as he watched the men leave. He opened his mouth to reply, but nothing came out.

"Amos?" I turned to my other friend. He surely would have some words of comfort to offer. He turned to me with the saddest eyes I had ever seen.

"We fight." The words came out with a pained croak. I slumped my shoulders. In my estimation, that was the last response I could hope for. He looked the part of a slave condemned to die. Coincidentally, I felt the same way. I buried my face in my hands. I could not bear the anguish in the expressions of those that stayed.

When the departures slowed and finally stopped, Gideon stepped forward. He addressed the much smaller crowd, "Thank you brave warriors who have chosen to stay and fight for your Creator. This...this is certainly an unexpected turn of events. I ask that you now take time to pray and meditate on our path forward. God is with us. We will be victorious. We may not know what that victory looks like. The path to victory may be more perilous than before, but the outcome will be the same. We will talk soon."

For a few stunned moments, after Gideon dismissed us, no one moved an inch. We simply stared as a collective group, straight ahead. It was as if the Midianites had raided all over again, taking almost everything we had. One by one, men started to go back to where they had made their camp for the night. Amos was first to move in our trio, Tabor followed and I kept my eyes fixed on Gideon. He eventually started towards his tent and I so wished I could follow him to hear what prayers he would offer up to this God that we were supposedly about to be slaughtered for. The momentary debate ended with me following Amos and Tabor, head held low.

Chapter 16

I could think of nothing else to do other than lie on my blanket and close my eyes. Tabor and Amos talked in hushed whispers but I could not imagine a combination of words that could be strewn together that would make me feel better. Even returning home now felt helpless. Surely the Midianites would be furious that we had stood against them in the first place. Bypassing military engagement would not be enough to satiate their bloodlust.

We had rebelled, and now certain death awaited us; either on the battlefield or in our homes. Or in my case, on the land where my home used to stand. I pulled the blanket up over my face, dismissing the idea of trying to find the strength to be optimistic. I would indulge in my self-pity and then reevaluate the situation afterwards. The slumber that dreams had disturbed the night before found me in the afternoon sun. I slept and I slept hard. I have no idea how long I had slept, but when I woke, it felt like it had been days. I stood and stretched, much to the surprise of Amos.

"Did you pray upon the matter?" he asked as I gained consciousness.

"As a matter of fact, I did not. I slept. Did you?" I asked with a hint of rebellion in my voice. It was unjustified, of course. It had not been Amos who had stirred this course of action. It all fell on my shoulders. Both of my friends were in this predicament because of me. I had to do something.

"I did. I heard nothing back." Amos said dejectedly.

"How convenient of our Lord." I said bitterly. "I'm going for a walk." I could see the concern on his face so I added, "There is no need to fear. I am not abandoning our post, nor am I seeking a drink. I just need to think and move." By the look on his face, I could tell that this offered no real assurances, but he relented and let me walk in solitude. I wandered over to Gideon's tent. The flaps were closed and several soldiers stood guard outside to prevent visitors. No words were exchanged but I stood and listened for a moment. It soon became apparent that he was in his tent, praying. He prayed with ferocity, if not confusion. I could not make out the specific words he was saying but the source felt betrayed and frightened of the day's outcome. This did nothing to comfort me and after a while, I continued my walk alone. The ground was littered with items that had been discarded by the men who had been here only hours before. There were weapons of varying quality, jugs, wineskins, and traveling gear. I could not find the rationale behind leaving such personal possessions in the dust but kept an eye out for anything that could be of use. I stopped when I saw a jug that appeared to be full on the ground. I knelt beside it and put it to my nose.

The sweet smell of wine filled my nostrils and I was overcome with temptation. I lowered the jug again and closed my eyes. What would one little drink hurt? What would one little drink help? Neither had a discernible answer so the question reverberated round and round in my head. I knelt there for an impossible amount of time when I felt a hand on my shoulder. The physical touch jolted me into the present. I stood in a panic and found Gideon behind me.

"It is not the developments that we had expected, is it?" He said with a slight smile on his face. Had he watched me struggling with the urge to down the jug of wine? He had to. I was the only one out here.

"Why say anything at all? If men wanted to leave, they would have. Why did you give them the option to walk away without consequence?" I said, exasperated.

"I gave you the same opportunity. Twice if I'm not mistaken."

"But you lost real soldiers. Soldiers who would have been vital to our mission. You traded viable fighting men for someone like me!"

"And I'd do it all over again, Ethan. I'd rather have you by my side than any of the men who left us. I meant it when I said you were right where you were supposed to be. Don't you see that yet? Why didn't you leave when you had the chance?"

I looked down at the ground and thought for a moment before looking into his eyes, "Because of you, Gideon. I didn't leave because of you?"

He smiled more broadly. "It wasn't me, Ethan. It was God. He speaks through me and we shouldn't waste our energy or time debating that. If you see something in me that inspires you, it comes from Him. Things will get worse before they get better. Anything worth accomplishing comes with great tribulation. The hurt you are feeling should bolster your conviction. It is evidence of belief. Do not lose heart. I am still here and not going anywhere. God's promises are more valuable than 22,000 men with swords. They are more valuable than 135,000 Midianites. It is hard to see from our perspective, but that doesn't make it less true."

I stumbled backwards blindly. "Please tell me you are randomly generating numbers. Please tell me you speak in hyperbole."

"We have taken great care to accurately gauge the number of men we have, I mean had, and the number of men we face. I do not pull numbers from thin air."

"So you are telling me that you think 10,000 Israelites will defeat 135,000 Midianites?" This was patently absurd. No sane individual could boast such claims.

"I said to take heart. Those will not be the numbers when we finally enter into battle. There is more to come. Do not fear." With those words, Gideon turned and made his way to a group of men nearby. He knelt with them and began talking. You could see the doubt and fear in their faces but Gideon commenced with his usual charm and grace. I felt a little better. He obviously had a plan. I did not trust God's promises but when Gideon promised it would not be 10,000 men against 135,000, I did believe. This obviously meant that he had a reserve army ready for reinforcements. I could not imagine it rivaling our initial numbers but if it offered Gideon, I would take it to heart as well.

* * * * *

Amos and Tabor noticed by my expression that my mood had been elevated since my departure.

"You didn't..." Amos started.

I looked at him with astonishment. "You think I found wine in the middle of this valley and then downed a jug?" I asked incredulously.

"I'm just asking. You seem different." Amos defended himself.

"Well, as it just so happens. I did. I found a big ol' jug of sweet red wine there for the taking. I will not lie, I almost took a drink. I did not, though. As I sat there debating with myself, Gideon walked up behind me. He reassured me that there were reinforcements on the way to take the place of those who left today."

Amos and Tabor smiled. Tabor enthusiastically asked, "That's what he said? He specifically said there would be reinforcements coming. How many?"

"Well, he didn't say that exactly. By his last census, we are down to 10,000 Israelites. We are up against 135,000 Midianites." Their faces dropped when the numbers were revealed. I couldn't stand to see the hopeless expressions so I continued quickly, "But he guaranteed that it would not stack up that way when we attack. Why would he be so self-assured if that did not mean more help was on the way?"

The looks of hopelessness turned to looks of trepidation. They were still not convinced this was a good thing, but they were both glad to see me happy again.

"We are going to be a part of something big. I can feel it." I said.

"Can you imagine me walking back into Rimmon as a hero and liberator? Who would have thought it?" Tabor said with a distant look in his eyes.

"Not me." Amos chided. "Do you remember the first time I met you?"

Tabor squinted his eyes in contemplation and finally relented, "No, I don't"

"You were not even a man yet if one would consider you one now. You and Ethan were barely waste-high to your parents. Apparently, you had both found some of Ethan's father's wine. There was a harvest festival and all the kids were running around playing. I couldn't find Ethan, but I heard his giggle from behind a house nearby."

"I don't remember this at all." Tabor interrupted.

"You will understand in a moment. Anyway, I came around the house and you and Ethan were finishing off a jug of wine. Ethan, you were quietly trying to roll a barrel over to the house but didn't have the balance to get it done by yourself. Tabor had to give you a hand. You were both trying to spy on a house. Upon further investigation, I noticed that there was a beautiful young woman getting dressed and you were trying to sneak a glimpse through the window. You were too drunk to maintain any semblance of balance and Tabor, you fell off a barrel, directly into a pile of goat dung. Ethan, you were laughing so hard you didn't even notice Tabor throwing the excrement at you. I just stood there, disgusted yet unable to turn away. The best part of the story was when the woman came running out of the house, barely dressed, to chastise you for spying on her in the first place. I believe I even got smacked a couple of times even though I had nothing to do with your attempted debauchery."

The three of us started laughing so hard, tears were streaming down our cheeks. It was at that moment that we heard the trumpets sound out again.

We all turned at the same time to find Gideon, once again heading up the hill to speak to us. Our laughter died in our throats and without speaking, we stood and walked towards the hill. The 10,000 men paled in comparison to the morning crowd. I tried to push the thought away and began to hope for word of reinforcements.

"Gentlemen, once again I must thank you for your bravery and support. I have had the honor of meeting so many of you and there was not one conversation I had where I walked away disappointed. Despite our numbers, we make a formidable force. We will not be reckoned with. Since I have had the privilege of meeting so many of you, I think it is only right that you take the time to meet with one another. This may seem unorthodox but listen carefully. I want you to leave your jugs, wineskins, and flasks where they are. Empty-handed, I want you to all line up along the river and wait for further instructions.

I looked at Amos and Tabor quizzically but obediently started to the river. All ten thousand men lined up along the western bank of the river as Gideon forded the waters. He faced the men. The men that always surrounded him paced back and forth behind us. An odd feeling washed over me.

"On my word, you will all take a drink from the river to signify our unity in moving forward. It is a minor gesture with significant implications. Your lives will never be the same after this moment in time."

It sounded ominous.

It sounded suspicious.

Doubt, once again, threatened me to the core.

Chapter 17

Amos stood to my left and Tabor to my right. We knelt down on the bank of the river and Gideon began to pray.

"Oh Heavenly Father. Please bless these men and keep them safe in our efforts to honor you. No matter their role in the upcoming days, please watch over them and fill their souls with your peace. Please bless us with understanding regarding your ways and keep us free of the grip of the enemy. Bless the water that runs before us and use it to cleanse us of our sins. We drink in honor of you, Oh Holy Creator."

Gideon knelt down to the water and took a drink. We followed his lead. Sensing the weight of the moment to my very core, I dipped my hands in the water as ceremoniously as I could. I gently raised the water to my mouth and took a drink. The cool, fresh water quenched my thirst in the heat of the day. I kept my eyes closed, oblivious to all those around me. I tried to repeat Gideon's prayer in my mind as I felt the water pour down my throat.

After a few moments, I leaned back and opened my eyes. Amos, Tabor, and I shared a quick glance and when Gideon stood, we stood as well.

"Men, Listen carefully to my words. For those of you that drank directly from the river, bypassing your hands, please take, five steps backward. For those that used your hands to bring the water to your lips, remain where you stand."

No one moved for a few moments as confused looks were shared amongst the men. Had we done something wrong? I frantically searched my recollection for a hint. Did he give us specific directions on how to drink from the river? I swore that he only said, take a drink from the river. If there were directions, had I done it wrong?

"This is no test and no one has done anything wrong. Those of you that drank directly from the river, bypassing your hands, please take, five steps backward."

It was as if Gideon had been reading my mind. His attempt at reassurance fell on deaf ears, though. Much to my horror, both Tabor and Amos took five, slow steps backward. Was this a way of dividing up our forces for strategic purposes? If so, I was not looking forward to being separated from my friends. I did not see the benefit of this strange organizational ploy. I looked once again to my left and right and noticed that almost everyone had sipped directly from the river. Panic crept up, once again and my heart started to race.

"For those of you still standing at the bank of the river, come stand behind me." Gideon shouted along the line of men. I felt defeated. I was being separated. The few who had chosen to drink as I did, crossed the shallow river and stood behind Gideon. Amos and Tabor donned a protective glare directed at me. They obviously did not like this separation either.

Gideon turned his attention to the thousands of men who had drunk directly from the river as I stood with the few that did not. "Men, you have served your God well. Your bravery and determination have given you great honor. You volunteered to fight the enemy of Yahweh. You stayed when it was easier to leave, against the odds. You are truly great men who have earned your spot in history. With that being said, I am no longer in need of your services. You may return to your homes with the knowledge that the Midianites will no longer be a threat to you or your families."

Cries and Furious Screams filled the other side of the bank from the men who had been dismissed. I looked at Amos and Tabor and they were arguing with each other but I could not hear what they were saying. They were gesturing wildly in desperation. I simply slumped my shoulders. I had made up my mind. Gideon had promised the Midianites, Israeli slaves. We were going to be delivered to them to live a life of servitude in agreement that the lands of Israel be free from their raids. I was just a lamb to be sent to the slaughter. I guess when Gideon saw how outnumbered we were, he realized all of this was pointless.

Gideon turned to us to speak. I didn't want to listen to a word he said, but I was curious about what my future would hold so I waited for his speech. I felt no need to look at him, though as he started.

"Men. God Almighty has chosen us, the select few to experience the victory that He will provide against the Midianites."

as a slave?

"I know this seems daunting. It seems impossible, but God has promised us victory and we shall have it." The old man who still seemed to be hanging around whispered something in his ear and Gideon continued. "We, three hundred men from the tribes of Israel, will defeat the Midianites and purify this land once again under Yahweh's dominion. Do not fear for your future. We will overcome."

He is still going to pretend that we are going to war? This was obviously a ruse and he was trying to placate us while he delivered us peacefully to the Midianites. Screams of anguish continued from the other side of the river and I looked beyond Gideon to witness the backlash of such an arbitrary way of selecting an 'army'.

Tabor and Amos had broken through the single line of Gideon's security and were screaming at our fearless leader. Gideon turned to face them.

"That is our friend!" Amos screamed at Gideon. "We are not leaving here without him. I don't know what foolhardy plan you think you are going to enact, but it will not include Ethan."

"And in what world is it ok to select an army based on the methodology of drinking water from a running river?!" Tabor screamed. I thought I saw tears forming in his eyes, but that couldn't be; that was just not Tabor. He didn't cry.

Behind our little scene, a few others were standing around, unable to believe that they had been relieved of their duties while a majority of the other 10,000 began to disperse and leave for home. Gideon, as he always did, looked at Tabor and Amos with an intensity that immediately made them halt their pleas.

"Amos, Tabor. Please listen to me. Your friend is under God's protection. You are not being sent home as a punishment. You did nothing wrong. You would have made great soldiers. Of that, there is not a doubt in my mind. Maybe one day, you still will if that is your desire. For this challenge, I have who I need standing behind me. Promises have been forged in the heavens that will keep them under a hedge of protection far beyond human comprehension."

Tabor stepped forward, tears now streaming from his eyes. It broke my heart to see this man agonizingly in front of me. He never took anything in life seriously and laughed his way through all of life's curses, all with a smile on his face. Now, he looked on the brink of death. "But I have so much to give. I have so much inside of me that I want to use to honor God." His words cracked in a desperate whisper. "Please. Let me stay and redeem myself for all of my sins. Let me..." his voice trailed off as the lump in his throat grew. How could anyone look into the bloodshot eyes and deny a man so willing to give his life for a noble cause?

Gideon, as he was prone to do, put his hand on Tabor's shoulder and with equal volume responded, "You have redeemed yourself, Tabor. Redemption comes in many forms. We do not all need to be on that battlefield for God to see us. Go in peace and know that he loves you. He wants what is best for you. Live a life that honors Him. God willing, you and Ethan, and Amos will all grow old together in a land free from eastern violence."

Tabor's head dropped and his body sobbed. It may not have been the answer that he wanted, but he was helpless to change it. He nodded weakly and Amos stepped forward and put his hand on his other shoulder. He turned his gaze to Gideon.

"That boy has invested his full confidence in you." Amos said as he nodded at me. "I hold you personally responsible for his safety." The words were spoken to intimidate, but they had no effect on Gideon.

"Ethan has placed his confidence in God, and for that, he will be protected. I am simply an earthly vessel for the divine message. I love Ethan as a brother and will do all that I can to keep him safe. For that, you have my word."

Amos remained stone-faced. "I thought I knew God. I have served him my whole life. I have searched my soul to try and understand what good can come from any of this, and for the life of me, it just seems like a suicide mission. I would have been as fierce a warrior for you as anyone out here. I hope you know what you are doing."

Gideon smiled, "I have no idea what I am doing. I will simply wait for God's instructions and try to follow them as faithfully as possible. As for your service, I have no doubts you are as fierce as they come. I do not claim to know God's will, but perhaps your path includes a different purpose. I wish you peace and a safe return home."

Amos grunted and he turned his attention to me. "Do you still wish to serve, Ethan?"

I looked at Amos and then at Tabor, lost and desolate. With tears brimming in my eyes I finally managed to say, "They can not know how everyone drank. I will claim otherwise and go home with you."

Tabor whipped his head around as if I had offended him. He had such pain in his eyes. He cried, "Why did you go with me all those times?"

I looked at him confused.

"Why did you go with me through all of my little mishaps and distorted adventures?"

"What do you mean?"

"All the times I went after a woman. All the times I chased a girl just to see if I could conquer her. All the times I let the drink determine how our night would end. All the dumb quests I embarked upon just to get my hands on something I shouldn't possess. All the misadventures that rankled your soul and went against your will. Why did you accompany me?"

"To be with you. It was all because of you. You are my friend."

"Friend. What is that to you? Is that a casual label or a badge of honor?"

"How dare you question your loyalty to you, especially in a time like now!"

"I'm not. I'm just asking you a simple question. Do you remember what you said to me so many years ago? We were drunk outside of Millian's winery. You looked at me and said you only wanted one thing. Do you remember what that was?"

"How could I possibly remember?"

"You said, you wanted nothing more than to die sober, doing something honorable. That was all that you wanted." Tabor uttered ferociously

"You remember that?" I said meekly

"It's a friend's job to remember stuff like that!"

"I am your friend, Tabor."

"If that is true, then stay here. Do this honorable thing that demands so much sacrifice. Win this battle, Ethan."

"How can I win this battle?" I asked in complete desperation.

"Not the war with the Midianites. Win YOUR battle, Ethan. That is all that I wish for you. Win your battle and return to me with honor and peace in your heart. That is all that I wish for."

Win my battle? What was he talking about?

"Stay safe, friend. I hope to see you again soon." Even though he knew I hated it, he embraced me and kissed me on the cheek.

"Please, Tabor. Keep your hopes up. This is not the end for you. You are one of my dearest friends and we will be together again soon." I said, determined to end this internal agony he was suffering.

Tabor nodded but could not find the words. Amos and Tabor both turned and slowly ambled away. I stared at them as they left, wishing

I could join them. Deep inside, it felt as if I could not though. I was tethered to Gideon for reasons I could not articulate.

Gideon wrapped an arm around my shoulders and led me back to the group of three hundred men who were doomed to stay. The men instinctively huddled together and waited to hear what was next. All the characteristics of my panic had slowly begun to subside. The tightness in my stomach, the racing heart, and the chest pains, all seemed to diminish as the hopelessness set in. I was destined to be here. It was my fate. It was over and there was nothing I could do about it. I wanted to be angry, but anger is an unearned emotion. I had earned this circumstance through all of my sinful behavior over the course of my life.

I looked around at the men who shared this assignment and there was a wide range of emotions on display. Some seemed even more impossibly eager. Others seemed frantic at the possibility of walking into battle against 135,000 enemies. Still, others seem to share my hopelessness at what lay ahead. As we waited to hear what Gideon had to say, I found myself wishing that I had plundered that jug of wine in the field.

At the very least, I didn't have to worry about crying in front of the men. All of my tears had dried up.

Chapter 18

I was alone. I felt more alone than the morning I settled into that cavern outside of Rimmon. I thought that was my lowest point, but this seemed worse. Then, I had no hope for a future. Since then, emotions had been stirred and hope took seed. Now my hope had been ripped away from me and there was nothing to take its place. We were instructed to gather the materials of the men that departed. We were specifically tasked with collecting as many ram horns, jars, and weapons as we could find.

I did my job without thought or passion. I just moved my body and did what I had to do. I found a couple of jars and one horn. Then, I stumbled upon some jugs that were left behind. The first two were empty and I was shocked at the disappointment that shot through me. The third was a pure victory. I found wine in the jug and without thought, began to chug it. I stopped after a bit to ensure that I had some for whatever lay ahead but it had the intended effect. It went right to my head and I started to feel 'normal' again.

As I struggled to show restraint and not finish what was left behind, I heard a voice behind me, "I know you. Rimmon, correct?"

I turned, panicked that I had been caught. The man stood tanned in the sun with curly brown hair and large hazel eyes. It took a few moments but I realized that he did look familiar. A beard covered his face where it hadn't before but I still could not place him.

"It is I, Rafal. I believe I found you in a cave outside of Rimmon."

"That is it!" I shouted involuntarily. "You saved....you found me in the cave and invited me to this place." The words came out more accusatory than I meant, but he took it in stride.

"Well, I didn't know this is what I was inviting you to, but yes. I did deliver the message. How are you, my friend?"

I shrugged, having no real answer that would benefit anyone.

"It is good to see you. You look a lot better than the last time I found you. Your wound seems to have healed a great deal. Despite our present circumstances, I am glad that you are here. It may not seem like it, but you are in a far better place than when I found you."

I snorted, uncertain of that assertion.

"Let us finish our scavenging and we can sup together by the fire." He said with a grin.

Since I had no one else on earth to converse with, I decided this would be the best I could do. I agreed and we continued to pick up the random materials that were left behind. As the sun began to descend in the sky, we found ourselves back in camp, in front of Gideon's tent. Several small fires had been started and men started to form awkward small groups. No one seemed to know each other so conversation was at a bare minimum.

A surprising amount of food had been left behind and it provided good portions for those of us who remained. I ate my fill for the first time that I could remember. When the food was gone, I looked around the fire. Rafal was just finishing up his meal and there were a couple of other men who had chosen our fire to sit around. The evening grew cool rather quickly, so we huddled closer together.

"Please forgive me, but I do not recall your name." Rafal said as he swallowed his last bite.

I took a drink from my jug, no longer compelled to hide my alcoholic intake. I was pacing myself because I did not know when and where my next drink would come from.

"There is no need to apologize. I am impressed that you recognized me at all. My name is Ethan. I do not feel like I properly thanked you for finding me that day. I appreciate your efforts in keeping me alive. Though, I fear it was a short-lived reprieve."

Rafal chuckled, "Fear not. We are as safe here as anywhere on earth. Have faith. I have known Gideon for quite some time and we are in good hands. In regards to your gratitude, it was nothing. I was simply blessed to be there when you needed me to be. That is how God works. People are placed in our lives when we need them most."

"And here you are again." I said, somehow believing him.

"Here I am again. Of course, you could be here to save me this time. One never knows the mysterious ways of the Lord. How do you fare now?'

The wine had taken effect so I answered, "I am ok. The uncertainty of our path weighs on me heavily but I am alive."

Rafal nodded towards the wine jug and I thought he was going to ask to partake, but instead, he said, "I would be careful with that. One never knows when we will be called into action and as you pointed out, we never know what lies ahead. Best to keep your wits about you."

I had been chastised and it stung. Admonishments from those closest to me came from a place of concern, but this felt somehow worse. "Point taken. I drink it sparingly." The lie slipped out far too easily.

"Can I ask you a question?" Rafal said after the moment hung heavily in the air.

"Of course." though I would rather you didn't, I thought.

"If an uncertain future causes you such angst, why did you choose to stay when you were given the opportunity to leave?"

It was a fair question. In fact, it was a question I had asked myself many times in the last day. "I guess I am a glutton for punishment."

Rafal laughed and the tension was eased. "If that is true, when all of this is said and done, I have a sister, Yaffa, you should meet who has yet to find a husband."

I laughed out loud.

"I guess I should have asked if you were in fact married before offering to give my sister away so casually." Rafal said, taking a sip of his water. I wanted to drink more wine but now I felt as if I were being carefully watched. The temptation was too strong and I decided to take a quick gulp.

"There was someone who I planned to marry but the Midianites assured me that no such pleasure was to be had. My entire family was murdered by their plundering hands. I guess that is the real answer to your original question. Returning home offers nothing for me."

"The Midianites can take our property and our family, but they can never steal our faith. There may be something there for you still. One never knows. Of course, you might like the Golan region. It is east of the Sea of Galilee and a lovely place to settle."

"I surmise that you have been there."

"My entire life. We have a lot of land to farm and raise sheep. We have been victim to Midianite raids as well but have managed to stow away enough to get by. When all this is said and done, you might want to visit."

"I might. This is my first time outside of Rimmon and it feels a shame to ignore everything else that was created." I said, knowing full well that I would probably never take him up on his offer.

"That is a refreshing attitude to witness. Most seem content to settle where they were born, never wishing to see new things." Rafal responded.

"Can you blame them? There may be much beauty in the world but there is also suspicion and violence for strangers who explore this land." I countered.

"True, but there are also wonderful people to meet and lands to see. It would be a shame to miss out on such opportunities for fear of what might happen."

I nodded. The circular argument was ruining the effects of the wine and I could see there would be no out-talking Rafal.

Just then, another man joined us by the fire, crossing his legs and holding his hands toward the flame. "Hello, fine men. How are you this beautiful evening?"

I had to look twice. This was no man, he was just a boy. His enthusiasm was evident and he was very handsome and muscular. I thought of all the men that we had lost and here sat someone barely old enough to get married.

"We are well, friend. I am Rafal, and this here is Ethan. It is a pleasure to make your acquaintance." Rafal said cheerfully.

"My name is Jether. It is very nice to meet you."

Rafal raised one of his eyebrows and inquired, "Jether, are you Gideon's son?"

"Yes. I don't go around shouting that because I wish to be treated no differently than the others, but Gideon is my father."

I looked up at him, "Did he give you a warning about how to drink the water?" I was just curious to see if there was going to be any nepotism involved.

Jether shook his head, looking a bit bewildered, "No, and I didn't see that coming. Let's just say family dinners would have been a little awkward if I had drunk directly from the river."

"You think he would have sent you home?" I said, filled with doubt.

"Oh yes!" The quickness of his answer led me to believe him. "My father is a man of his word. If that was the message he received from God, he would have sent me home in a heartbeat."

"You are quite young to be a soldier, are you not?" Rafal said with ill intent.

Jether smiled easily, "I am young, but I am fierce. In fact, while you old men grow weary in battle, I will still be going strong!" Jether said while pounding his chest for emphasis.

I laughed despite myself, "You can carry our canes then."

Jether chuckled. He was very easy to like and I could see the resemblance between him and Gideon, in personality and appearance.

"It has been a long, confusing day. I believe that I will retreat to my blanket and try to get some sleep." I concluded.

Rafal nodded and closed his eyes. He began talking low and I realized that he was praying, as Amos had done back home. I could not understand everything that he had said but I was able to glean small snippets and realized that he was praying for me. At first, I was slightly offended that he thought I needed his prayers, but then I realized that I could use all the prayers I could get.

The wine sent my mind drifting randomly from topic to topic as I lay on my blanket and closed my eyes. I missed Padma with all of my being but the mention of Rafal's sister sent me down another road. What if there was someone out there for me? What if this was not the end of my story? Could I rebuild a life, one that was better than before? Those questions rattled around in my head as I drifted off to sleep.

* * * * *

There is plenty of evidence to show throughout my history that when I drink, I do not wake up in the middle of the night. The Midianites raiding Rimmon, and having to be physically carried at the start of our march, are just a couple of examples of how soundly I slept while was inebriated. This night was different. I rolled over when something stirred but then tried to remain as still as possible. What I saw in the dying light of the fire shook my nerves.

Gideon and another man were quietly escaping the camp. They walked as quietly as they could away from the sleeping men under cover of night, leaving the rest of us here to die. Is this how it was to be done? Were we being left here so the Midianites could take us in the dead of night in exchange for Gideon's life?

If that were the case, so be it. I was so devoid of any hope, I just lay there and waited for my fate. I took the opportunity to finish the wine that I had been 'partaking in sparingly'. Only this time I gulped it with full abandon. I was going to be taken prisoner in the dead of night, I was going to do my best to ensure that I did not remember any of it.

I looked up at the sky and stared at the stars. There were so many. If I had not viewed them through blurry vision, maybe I could find some motivation in their beauty. I tried to think of reasons to live, willing myself to stay awake and enjoy my last few moments of freedom because when the wine would hit me and I would close my eyes, it would be all over.

Amos. Amos could be a reason to live. But he was sure to find a wife soon and raise a family. There would be no time for someone like me. Tabor would go back to whatever Tabor does, though I wondered if Tabor had really changed. It seemed like it as he left. As much as he appreciated his friends, lying here now, alone in the Jazreel Valley with an army of men coming to either kill him or enslave him, it just didn't seem like enough.

"Get up!" a voice screamed in the night. The Midianites had arrived to take us away.

Chapter 19

"Get up! For the Lord has given you victory over the Midianite hordes!"

I knew the wine had taken effect because this made no sense to me. I know I slept through a lot but there was no way that I had slept through a victory over 135,000 hostile combatants. The levels of this trickery were impressive. Men began to stir and Rafal shook me awake.

"Make Ready!" He said as he began to grab a spear that he had kept near him. I don't know if he plundered it or if it was his, but I know that I would have felt better owning a weapon that would have put more distance between me and my enemy. I stood up and wobbled a bit. I hoped that instability would be interpreted as grogginess from slumber but I was paranoid my drunkenness would be revealed.

"They sleep on the other side of the hill and now is the time to take them. All the bravery that led you to this spot is needed tenfold now. Grab your weapons and follow me." Gideon said. Despite the darkness, the moon revealed the fire in his eyes. He had his leather armor on and sword in hand. He looked like a warrior. I looked like an impoverished farmer who had abandoned his lot in life. I grabbed my knife and reached for the jug. It was empty. I should have kept some to bolster my bravery when needed but I was never one for moderation.

Rafal put his hand on my back and urged me forward. Someone was counting somewhere off in the distance. When they reached 100, they were separated from the rest of us. Just what we needed. Let's take 300 soldiers and divide them up even smaller against such a substantial force. The counting began again. It ended at 100 again and they were separated as well. I found myself in a group with Gideon and Rafal and I thanked Yahweh for such a small blessing.

I stumbled just a bit and Rafal steadied me. I focused on Gideon and watched the way that he moved. Each and every movement was filled with efficiency and purpose.

"Each man should have a torch in one hand and a jar in the other!" Men scrambled about to get the provisions that were demanded.

I once again was confused by these directions. How were we to fight with a jar and a torch? We were not the best armed 'army' if you could even call us that. Why would we handicap ourselves with a seemingly useless item like a jar? Even the torch seemed frivolous. If the point was to attack in the dark, illuminating our approach seemed counterintuitive.

A jar and a torch were shoved into my violently shaking hands and I squeezed them tight, desperate not to drop either. Men ran around, using the lit torches to light the dormant ones. I took deep breaths to recalibrate my state of mind. A frenzy of thoughts rushed forward as I tried to clear my mind. I watched Gideon trying to steal his bravado and confidence.

Gideon stood in front of the three divisions of men and began to speak again.

"This group will circle around to the north of the camp." He pointed to a man who was designated on the spot to lead the men around the entire camp opposite them.

"This group will line the western edge of the camp." He pointed to another man who had to stand a full foot taller than me, a real soldier. He nodded solemnly while he seemed to calculate the path in his mind.

"We will line the southern border of the camp. This leaves their only path to escape to the east. The river should hinder them. **Keep your eyes on me. When I come to the edge of the camp, do just as I do. As soon as I and those with me blow the rams' horns, blow your horns, too, all the entire camp and shout, 'For the Lord and for Gideon!'**"

I grabbed the Rams horn on my left side, opposite my knife. Somehow, despite the copious amounts of wine I had ingested, I had kept these two items by my side. I shocked myself by saying a quick prayer of thanks to Yahweh.

I am no expert on the moon and stars but I could tell by their placement that we were nearing the exact middle of the night. We began to trudge up the hill as I tried to maintain the fickle balance between liquid brave and being out of my mind. I thought of my father, Padma, checkers, Amos, Tabor, anything to keep my mind off of what was actually happening. The idea of actually striking another man in anger was so foreign to my nature, it was beyond my comprehension.

The grass was wet with dew and in the back of my mind, I hoped somewhere that fleece was dry. I still doubted that Yahweh would lower Himself to the trials and tribulations of such men but I had trepidatious confidence in Gideon that good things would happen.

When we approached the top of the hill, Gideon handed his torch to the old man who had traveled with us. I noticed that the old man did not even have a weapon on him and wondered what use he could provide to our extremely abridged army. Gideon lay on his stomach and inched his way to the crest of the hill. He watched carefully.

What was he looking for?

After some time passed, he slid backward, stood, and ran to us. He took the torch back from the old man.

"They are changing their guards. Now is the time to act! May God protect you and keep you safe. Remember above all else that he is here with us tonight!"

We all walked as quietly as possible up the hill. I dropped the jar and immediately fell to the ground in a frenzied panic. My hands searched the damp grass until I felt something solid. I was falling behind and though a part of me did not mind this, I knew it would not do. I picked up the jar and caught up with Rafal who gave me a comforting glance.

We made it to the ridge and stood far atop the Midianite camp. My heart sank. There were more tents than I had ever seen in my entire life. Within those tents were multiple men. I thought back to the time I first saw the size of our army and was struck by how this one before us dwarfed our original gathering. Even if God was with us, there simply could be no way that we would see the light of day as victors. Even if I killed ten men, a hundred more would overtake me. The numbers kept playing in my mind and I could not rid myself of this impending doom that I felt.

With the torch in his left hand and jar in his right, he held the ram's horn between his lips. I tried to mimic his stance, but it was hard to balance the three items. He blew the horn and ripped open the silence of the night. Horns began to blow from all directions it seemed and I joined in. I placed the jar on the ground so that I could get a better grip on my horn

The acoustics of the valley and the three hundred horns made quite an intimidating cacophony of chaos, I had to admit. When all the breath was expelled from my lungs, Gideon raised the jar high above his head and thrust it to the ground. Others followed and the destruction of the pottery only added to what must have seemed like a confusing cluster of advancing, angry people.

I followed with what I hoped would be enough force to destroy the sturdy jar in my hand. It shattered at my feet and a shard whipped into my shin within moments, I could feel the blood start to trickle down my leg.

Please let that be the only mark of this battle that lay ahead.

"A sword for the Lord and for Gideon!" The shouts echoed throughout the valley and I panicked as I could not find my voice.

I looked over at Rafal who was screaming the words. I tried again and a pathetic yell escaped my lips. I tried again and found a volume I had never accessed before. Even the wailing I emitted upon the discovery of my father and Padma paled in comparison to the shout that I submitted to the night.

Below us, the camp exploded into a chaotic, rambunctious frenzy of activity. The Midianites emerged from their tents in a panicked state.

They ran, with no destination, they simply sprinted this way and that. Gideon blew his horn again, so we followed suit.

Why were we not taking advantage of the confusion? I know that I had doubted Gideon's strategy from the very beginning but this appeared to be the perfect time to strike. Why take the time and effort to surprise them and then commence watching from far above? I saw no point in surprising them only to become a bystander.

I turned my attention from Gideon to a Midianite soldier below. I picked one randomly to follow since apparently, that was our only role here. He had a spear in hand and inexplicably ran up to another Midianite and impaled him. The grotesque violence made my stomach curdle and I feared that I would vomit yet again. The blood oozed from his body and there was a pained expression in his face as he fell to his knees. From behind the aggressor, another Midianite raised his sword and brought it down. He struck a glancing blow off the scalp of the initial aggressor, forcing the blade into his shoulders. The soldier with the spear turned, but could not free his weapon. Another blow from the sword ended his life. I switched my attention to the man with the bloodied sword and he soon found another Midianite to dispatch of.

I could not fathom how they did not see that they were killing one another. I felt a perverse joy at watching our enemies murder their own but still felt as if we were plundering an opportunity. They would soon realize that the source of the chaos originated far above them and they would have to notice the torches that lined the camp on three sides.

Time crept by as the fervor only intensified. I looked at the river from the east and saw thousands of Midianites fording the ice-cold waters. They were either running for their lives or planned to circle back and attack us from behind. If that were the case, we would have no chance. We were only a hundred men and our paltry reinforcements were spread all around the hills.

I made a move towards Gideon to ask if we should prepare for a counterattack but Rafal put his hand on my shoulder. By the light of his torch, I could see that there was a peace about him. He had the hint of a grin on his lips.

"Just watch. Witness the Glory of our Father in Heaven as he purifies this land." I settled back into my position. Only then did it finally occur to me why Gideon had been so convicted about his role in all of this. I felt confidence begin to creep in and I found that it was definitely a feeling I could get used to.

Years of self-doubt and shame were all I knew but here I was. One of three hundred blessed individuals who actually was granted the privilege of watching the divine work. After a while, my feet began to ache and I desperately wanted to sit but I chastised myself for this impulse. Few have ever seen battle and their only complaint is that they had to stand for too long. It was a problem that I would joyfully endure.

The mesmerizing pandemonium lasted so long that the sun began to throw its light from the horizon beyond the river. It illuminated a steady stream of Midianites who were dispersing in all directions once they cleared the natural barrier.

The only scare we got was when a few Midianites approached us in a crazed hysteria. It took a bit to realize they were not advancing, only trying to escape. They were immediately killed by our men. It was the closest I had been to death and empathy flooded my soul. Seeing the men brought down in front of me was a stark reminder of what the end goal was. I forced myself to think about how these were the same people who had kept the Israelites living in fear and poverty to ease my conscience.

Eventually, the sounds of violence were reduced to a clatter of swords touching or a groan from a death blow, but silence then followed. The sun rose on an army camp that was completely decimated.

Cheers from our men on the three sides of the camp erupted and I felt the compulsion to join in. Gideon just smiled and raised his hand in victory.

"Rafal, inform the other two divisions to meet back at our camp," Gideon commanded.

"Yes, Gideon." Rafal was off. I remembered how he looked as he sprinted away from my cave once realizing I was no longer a danger to myself. No wonder Gideon had picked him. When Rafal was presented with a mission, he went about it expediently.

We descended the hill in celebration. I was filled with such joy that I could ignore the headache that was approaching and shaking my hands. I had survived my first 'battle' and the only wound I had was at the hands of a clay jar.

Rafal returned with the other two hundred men and we gathered around Gideon.

"What you witnessed tonight will be written about and discussed throughout history. You should each feel honored to have been a part of it. There is a message in this that I want you to understand. Each of you faced hardships and pain to get to this point. You felt doubt and despair. You thought it was hopeless. But remember this, all things are possible with God. I don't know if there is any evidence in the world that would convince you of this if you still doubt."

"Praise be to God!" the men began to shout. Some fell to their knees and wept. I simply bowed my head. I still was not articulate enough to find competent words, so I just kept repeating, thank you, God, over and over.

Gideon raised his hand again and the men went silent. "Our job is not over. We all saw how many of the Midianites, Amalek, and others escaped beyond the river. Many generations before we were punished for not finishing the mission. We can't let our oppressors regroup and continue to slaughter our people. They will not evacuate our land and count it as a loss. They will return with a vengeance so we move forward. Do not let this diminish the victory you saw tonight. God is still with us and will provide."

"Gideon, should we restock with the bounty that lies in the dirt of the Midianite camp?" A man asked.

"Only the food. Do not plunder their weapons. We have all we need."

Some of the men looked disappointed. Watching what unfolded with the superior arms of the Midianites offered a profound temptation to those of us who only carried knives, clubs, and hoes.

"If we are to continue to show God's power, we do not need weapons made of iron. The world will then say, 'of course they defeated them. They had weapons forged in iron that the world had never seen before. No, we must be conquerors with what we have."

Most of the men cheered but there were a few who wanted nothing more than to have some of those weapons that the world had never seen before. I know that I would have felt better with one, but I relented.

Gideon continued, "Rafal, You are to go throughout the hill country of Ephraim, saying '**Come down to attack the Midianites. Cut them off at the shallow crossings of the Jordan River at Bethbarah.**' Take ten men with you and depart now. Is that understood?"

"Yes, Gideon. It would be an honor." He went amongst the men and selected a few. I was simultaneously relieved and disappointed that he had not selected me. I understood of course. I was an unimposing figure with such little experience. I often did not know how to conduct myself around others and knew I would not be a good recruiter.

The euphoria from a violence-free victory, aside from Midianite on Midianite slaughter, was tempered by the fact I hoped this would be the end of the campaign. I had done something I never thought I would have the courage to do. I didn't know how much I had left to give.

Chapter 20

The men were off and the rest of us went down to the Midianite camp to retrieve any food that was left behind. The thrill of the 'battle' had begun to wear off and exhaustion was beginning to set in. I found some fruit and dried meats that would serve me well. I entered one of the larger Midianite tents and began to look around for supplies. I found another sack and some extra linens and tunics. I had never had a surplus of clothing before and became excited at the thought of being able to change clothes on a regular basis.

Then I saw it. In the corner were two large jugs. I stood in the tent and stared at them. I shouldn't even investigate. I should just let them sit where they were. If ever there was a time to stop this cycle of madness, it was here and now. I felt purpose and hope for the first time since I could remember. There was nothing in those jugs that held what I didn't already know. I stood there, transfixed on the ground, staring at the jugs.

I was to return home a conquering hero. I would rebuild my life. I might even stop by Golan and introduce myself to Rafal's sister. What was her name? Yaffa? It didn't matter what I did, I just knew that nothing good would come from walking over to those jugs and picking them up.

So I did. I smelled the contents and my worst fears were confirmed. It was wine. They were completely full. Without thought, I placed the jugs in my newfound sack and placed my new wardrobe on top of them, away from potentially prying eyes. I would not drink now. That was all I could promise myself. I quickly walked out of the tent and hated myself for feeling comforted by the knowledge that I had the wine as a 'backup'. I was sober now and hoped to stay that way.

When I exited the tent, Gideon stood across from me. We made eye contact and I wondered if he knew. How could he? The tent flap was closed and there was no way for him to see my theft. I was being paranoid. He walked over to me with a smile on his face.

"I am proud of you Ethan. I know how difficult this has been for you."

Was he talking about the wine or this fight?

"I know that you are not a fighting spirit but when the Lord called, you answered." He put his hands on my shoulders and gave them a squeeze. My knees buckled a bit, partly from guilt at what I had just done, partly because I desperately craved the praise he was offering. "Now, we begin the next part of our journey. I see you have increased your inventory quite a bit. This is good. For the next part of our journey, we travel by camel. Secure one from the camp and meet back at our original checkpoint. Next, we head to the Jordan River." He gave me a pat on the back and was off.

It was not over.

That was my fear, that we would chase the remaining Midianites and engage once more, only this time, we might actually have to fight. I debated opening one of the jugs and taking a quick swig but was able to quell the desire and just headed back to where I camped with Rafal the night evening before. I was happy I was not picked to alert the people of Ephraim but would miss my new friend. It appeared I was destined to go about this alone.

I sat down by my other sack and stirred the fire a bit to take the chill out of the morning air. I began to shake and had the urge to break down into tears. Now that things had settled a bit, I was able to reflect on what we had done overnight. Gideon could tell I was in dire straits and sat next to me.

"How are you holding up, Ethan?"

"I'm fine." I lied. "I just am a little nervous about our next steps. What is in store for us next?"

"Well," Gideon started, poking the fire a bit, "We did not find the two Midianite commanders that we had hoped to defeat. Oreb and

Zeeb have escaped. If we do not kill them, we are just in as much trouble as we were before. They are insatiable men who are bent on our destruction."

"I just don't understand. If we are all God's children, how can the slaughter of an entire people be considered holy? I know I am the furthest thing from a warrior, but it does not sit right with me."

Gideon seemed to ponder this for a moment. "Unfortunately, God needs to get our attention from time to time. The Israelites have grown weary and lazy. Make no mistake about it. Our Creator is a loving God, but he is also jealous. He does not wish to be worshiped alongside other so-called deities. If our laziness in worshiping Him was the only issue, who knows what course would have been necessary but the Midianites forced this course. They have corrupted our people and our traditions while forcing us into poverty. Do you so quickly forget what sent you here? What are you returning home to?"

I shook my head. I was not used to being chastised by Gideon and it shamed me to a deeper level. "I have nothing to return to. They have killed the only people that I loved. I have not forgotten this, but I am also not prone to vengeance either."

"You can call it vengeance, or you can deem it an awakening of your spirit. We are to return to the ways of our Lord. With those ways comes peace and harmony. This excursion is a simple method for returning our people to their rightful place." Gideon said, his eyes now boring into my soul.

I shifted uncomfortably. "I just wish I could hear his voice one time. Then I would be filled with the conviction that you possess."

"You think it is that simple? You think that by hearing God's voice, it all becomes clear. I fought him tooth and nail, despite hearing his voice. I am not a soldier either, Ethan, lest you forget. I was simply available to be used as a tool of Yahweh. There are other examples that can bring you comfort. It's all in the Holy Word. When Moses led our people from Egypt, do you think he quickly jumped to his feet and eagerly set about doing God's work?"

"I'm embarrassed to say that I am not familiar with Israelite history. I am not an educated man." I said, blushing just a bit at this admittance.

"Moses was told to tell the Pharaoh to let our people go. His response was that he was not a good public speaker. He had a speech impediment that he used to hide from God's will. God chose to use him anyway. We can't decide who God will call on to demonstrate His power, we can only be ready when that call is made. It is why we must keep our wits about us and forever listen for His word. He does not call the best and brightest. He calls the weak and broken."

Was this another shot at my drinking? Was Gideon telling me that I must abstain from the wine so that I could be ready for God when needed? All of this was too much. If God called the weak and broken, why didn't he just do it himself? He obviously did not need me! The Midianites killed themselves. They would have done that if I was passed out by the fire, back home, or nowhere at all. It didn't matter that I was standing on that hill.

Stop. Breathe. Gideon was staring at me. I had to rid myself of this shameful self-ridicule. It was not productive. I tried to remember the feeling of elation as I stood there and watched our victory. Was I not going to be forever grateful to be a party to such a historic event? I was too quick to forget such things.

"It is important to pray, Ethan. It is also important to still your mind and listen." I will leave you to get yourself ready to move again.

I stared at the fire and tried to pray. The words came difficult at first, but then a stream of consciousness began to form.

Here's my heart Lord; for the things I covet must be hidden. The things you promise should be presented in the light of day. I detest the secrets I hold. They are a barrier to you. Please remove the urges I have and give me the desires of my heart.

I closed my eyes to listen and lay back on my blanket. I don't know how long I lay there, but I heard nothing. My thoughts inevitably kept going back to the wine that was in my newfound sack of goods. If I was to hear God, I was going to have to overcome this obsession. I wish I could say that moment was an epiphany, but it was not. I heard nothing that day.

Chapter 21

In the absence of human companionship, I developed quite a fondness for my new camel. It was female, so I named her Valencia. It was a curious beast. Granted, I did not have a lot of experience with animals, but I loved her just the same. We began our journey and I was able to stave off the desire to dive head-first into the jugs of wine. Of course, I did not leave them behind, they just swayed back and forth on the right side of Valencia as we trekked through the land, headed towards the Jordan River.

The journey took a few days and word kept trickling back to us regarding how the people of Ephraim had risen up and wreaked havoc upon the retreating Midianites. Every report was promising and I harbored hope that we could avoid the confrontation that I had been dreading since this all began.

The land turned green and lush as we approached the river. After days of rigorous travel, I was glad to make a more permanent camp again. On the third day of sitting by the river, I had grown antsy and wished for some sort of development to occupy my mind. I had done little prayer and even smaller amounts of listening for God. I had given up hope that I would ever hear God. This frustration was offset by the return of Rafal to our ranks.

"Ethan, it is good to see you, my friend. How do you fare?"

"I am well. How were your travels? I hear you were once again successful in your recruitment to the cause."

"I was blessed to encounter men who had their ears opened by God. They were quite eager to rid the land of the Midianites. They were as motivated as we were. I was also able to swing by Golan and see my family once more. Yaffa told me to tell you hello. She is quite eager to meet you."

I blushed again at his forward banter. "I sincerely doubt that you would want someone like me to be a part of your honored family." I meant this earnestly. I could only imagine what his opinion of me was. He met me as I was attempting to end my own life. Since he has known me, I have been inebriated a majority of the time. How he could offer his sister's hand to me was beyond comprehension.

Rafal looked shocked, "When I look at you, I see a man transformed by Yahweh. You have come a long way in a short time. Do not belittle yourself. In the moments I met you, did you ever think that you would stand, towering above a conquered people?"

"I did not. Of course, they conquered themselves more than I did." Rafal snorted a short laugh and patted me on the back.

"Again with the self-shaming. You are a key part of God's plan and there is much more in store for you. Just be ready to answer the call when necessary."

"You sound like Gideon." I responded.

"Gideon is a brilliant man. He sounded more like you when this all began. He was as confused as anyone to be asked to lead men against our enemy. He just learned how to listen and have faith."

"So what do you think happens next? Will we have to meet Oreb and Zeeb in combat? Real combat?"

"You ask many questions, my friend. All will be revealed in time. I do not know what the future holds. When I try to figure it out, it only leads to bad places in my head so I have learned to live in the moment. Imagine this. I have made a new friend, we are sitting beside a beautiful rushing river while the sun rises in the east. We have all but conquered the people who have kept us in poverty all of our days on this earth. There is a cool breeze on a warm day. What else could we ask for?"

"You speak the truth, Rafal. Not to mention, I have a new friend. Meet Valencia." I said as I smoothed the hair on my camel's neck.

"This is my replacement?" Rafal said with a sly smile on his face. "You need more human companionship, my friend."

"Maybe. But look at those big, beautiful brown eyes. I've never owned an animal before. I've grown to be quite close to her." I countered.

"You are in more trouble than I thought." Rafal said and set about to make our fire.

I turned to Valencia and whispered to her that he was just jealous. Just then, people in our camp began to stir and a loud whispering began to emerge from the ranks. Someone was approaching from the east.

Gideon blew his ram's horn and we gathered around him. We could see riders off in the distance and my heart began to race. It had been a good day, I was now in a panic that it would all be ruined by an unexpected raid. Gideon did not seem alarmed, though, so I tried to calm my nerves.

"Remember, have faith in the Lord. He is good." Rafal whispered. I said a prayer of thanks that he was back. As the riders approached, it became obvious to Rafal who they were.

"They are from the tribe of Ephraim. They responded to the Lord's call."

It was obvious who the leader of the tribe was. He wore armor that was more expensive than anything that I had ever seen or could hope to own one day - not that I wanted to be in a position to wear armor ever again.

Gideon embraced the man and kissed him on the cheek. The leader of the Ephraimites did not look happy. He beckoned a soldier from behind him and a sack was presented to Gideon. Still, no words had been spoken.

The leader of the Ephraimites, stuck his hand in the sack and pulled out a severed human head, and flung it to the ground. The grotesque vision of the human head sent waves of nausea through me. My stomach was still weak from the past abuse of alcohol and I was constantly living in danger of vomiting at the least upsetting events. The leader of the Ephraimites pulled out another severed, bloodied by the neck, eyes bulging almost out of its skull. He threw it on the ground next to Gideon's feet.

"What is this that you have done to us, not to call us when you went to fight against Midian? So that was the source of their anger. They wanted in on the initial surge of fighting. This seemed pretty petty in my estimation. We had a common enemy and now they were all but vanquished. Who cared about the credit when all glory was supposed to go to God?

Gideon stepped forward and I was curious to see how he would respond to their anger. He had mastered almost every personal interaction I had been privy to since I met him, but this seemed a precarious situation. He cleared his throat and responded.

"What have I done now in comparison with you? Is not the gleaning of the grapes of Ephraim better than the grape harvest of Abiezer? God has given into your hands the princes of Midian, Oreb and Zeeb. What have I been able to do in comparison with you?"

The leader of the Ephraimites thought for a moment, without expression and then a slow smile crept across his face. Gideon had done it again. He had used his self-deprecating persona to dismiss the tensions that were so evident only moments before.

"Then we share this victory over our enemy together!" The man yelled. A cheer from both sides arose from the ranks. There were pats on the backs and embraces from men who knew victory in battle. I smiled and embraced Rafal. I would be going home soon. I pictured walking into Rimmon, word of our battlefield glory preceding me. Would I be cheered? Would people line the streets to get a glimpse of one of their own, amidst the famed three hundred soldiers who liberated the Israelites?

We sat in communion with our brothers from the tribe of Ephraim and celebrated what I interpreted to be the end of this war. Rafal sat next to me and talked of home and how much he missed it. I could not relate to such sentiments but I allowed him to go on and on. Wine flowed freely but I felt as if I were being watched by Gideon and Rafal so I did not partake. Many times I debated taking my private stash and going off on my own to have a few drinks but desperately fought this urge.

My emotions were getting the best of me and I started to become overwhelmed by the activity and socialization. My mind was obsessed with what was in my sacks and I cursed myself for not being able to enjoy the moment. I thought about my father and Padma while Rafal went on and on. I had to hide the tears that were threatening to come.

Suddenly, even though I did not miss home, I longed to be there nonetheless. At least there, I could isolate myself and not be required to perform this idle small talk with people I would never see again. At least the next time I set foot upon my land, I would not have to worry about another Midianite raid. I started to dream of rebuilding and living a life by myself, beholden to no one.

Chapter 22

I awoke in the middle of the night, sweat pouring from my forehead. My jaws had been clenched and my whole body was tense. I had a dream that I was hiding behind the front, ready to join the battle with the other men. I looked out over the Midianites and I quickly told Gideon that I had forgotten my knife and I must retrieve it before we advanced.

He looked at me with profound disappointment in his eyes and said nothing. He knew the real reason I was retreating. I got to my sack and found the wine. I downed the entire jug as fast as I could. I lay on the ground, mind drowning in the alcohol. I glanced up and saw the Midianite forces overtake our own. They were now advancing toward me. I was helpless. I could not move my arms or legs. I lay there, drunk, ready to be slaughtered by the very Midianites we had worked so hard to erase from the face of the earth. One of the Midianites, face dirty and yellow teeth bared, raised his sword and was about to bring it down on me to end my misery, I jerked awake under my blanket.

The dream had felt so real and held so much shame, it took a moment to gather my bearings. I looked around and noticed that everyone else was still sleeping. I pulled the newly acquired sack towards me and hid it under my blanket. I moved so carefully and slowly, that it would have been comical to anyone who happened to be watching. Underneath my blanket, I opened my jug and carefully poured it into one of the smaller wineskins. I placed it in my tunic and slowly rose. I took a deep breath of the chilled midnight air and walked towards the river, which I could hear somewhere behind me.

I sat on the bank and watched the black water rush by. I had to be careful near the rapids. I looked around one more time to see if anyone had followed me. I was alone. Finally, alone. I tipped the wineskin to my lips and let the warmth of the wine fill my stomach. I was not cut out for the role of hero. I would always be this way. I was a hopeless drunkard with nothing to offer God. I took another drink and the familiar light-headedness carried me away. I felt peace and serenity for the first time in days.

Once I got back home, there would be no one to disappoint. There would be no one to judge my indiscretions. That was how I wanted to live. Being near God had its moments. Long term, I would never be able to live the straight and righteous path. I drank until the sun began to crest the horizon. I felt content with my plan. Now, all I had to do was wait for Gideon to thank us for our services and dismiss us back home. I put my hands into the cold, river water and splashed it on myself to wake myself up. I stood, balanced myself, and headed back to my blanket. Upon my return, I woke up Rafal.

He sat up and rubbed his eyes. "Are you alright, Ethan?"

"Yes. I thought I heard something in the night and I went to check it out. I got distracted and ended up by the river. I have just been sitting there thinking."

"Oh." was all Rafal said. I noticed he was looking at my blanket. Sticking out from under the cloth was the jug of wine that I had snuck into hours before. My face got hot and the relief that I had felt dissipated into embarrassment. I cleaned up my area and prayed that he would not say anything to me. I had filled up my wineskin with water and went over to my camel to give her some. She licked my hands with her coarse tongue while I poured water over them. Her eyes did not judge me. Perhaps I did need human companionship. I felt like a camel that I had known just under a week was my new best friend.

The Ephraimites began to awaken and orders were given to return home. By afternoon, it was just the original three hundred soldiers. As the day lengthened, I became impatient and wondered what was taking Gideon so long. I debated going to him and asking him to be relieved of my duty since I was obviously no longer needed, but I resisted this urge.

As the sun began its descent, Gideon finally called us together. "Men, we must move on. In discussing the state of the Midianites with one of our messengers, it was revealed to me that 15,000 troops are still out there. We are to head north and end this campaign. We will rest in the city of Succoth. There, we will continue on until the two Midianite Kings, Zebah and Zalmunna are dead. No Israelite is safe until they are dead. They are like cornered beasts who will attack out of fear and spite and this could undo all the glory that we have worked so hard to bring to God."

My stomach reeled again. How was this still not over?

"Gentlemen, we have been spared in battle so far, do not expect to in the future. We will have to fight in the next engagement, but remember God's promise. The Midianites will be handed over to us. We will be victorious. Do not let your faith and bravery waver now. We are almost done with what we have been called to do. Stay strong!"

This is what I get for praying. I pray for peace and that my struggles are taken from me and that I am rewarded by being sent off to fight. I am to partake in violence, the very thing I have tried to avoid my entire life. I went back to the blanket and finished off the jug of wine without concern for who saw it. This rebellious behavior was met with looks of disappointment from all around me. Rafal looked heartbroken. I threw the empty jug on the ground in fury and tied the sack that still had the other jug around Valencia. If I was going to be forced to fight, I would do it my way.

The wine hit hard later that night as we rode our camels north. I was thankful that I did not have to walk or else I would have been stumbling all over the path. Of course, I did lean a little too dramatically this way or that way on top of my camel every now and then but was able to maintain my grip on the reins. Where there was nervous optimism on our trip to the Jordan River, silent tension settled in on our trip to Succoth. In fact, the only talking came from Gideon

who had begun the practice of praying over us one by one. When I saw
that he was headed toward me, I began to plot what I was going to say.

Get away from me, your prayers are as useless as this God we serve!

Save your prayers from someone who believes in them!

I've had enough of this talking to God - I'll serve the wine in my jug!

Of course, none of those sentiments emerged when he approached
me. He directed his camel to walk side by side with me and extended
his right hand towards me. I just lowered my head and tried to see one
of everything.

"Oh great and glorious Father in heaven. Please fill Ethan with
your love and make him feel your presence, more profoundly than
ever before. He is hurting in spirit, Lord, and needs the hope that can
only come from You. He has a servant's heart so please inspire him to
become a leader of men and honor You and bring glory to Your Name.
Please heal the pain inside of him and reveal to him a strength that he
never knew he possessed. You will be done, Lord. Amen."

Gideon said nothing more and moved on. The words had a
surprising impact on me. The temper tantrum I wanted to throw was
dismissed and I found myself ruminating on his prayer. How was my
internal pain so visible to him? How did he know I was hurting? I gave
in and said a short prayer.

Lord, please listen to Gideon's prayer. His prayers are better than
mine.

That was all I had to say to God.

* * * * *

Succoth

We arrived in Succoth, in the middle of the region of the tribe of Gad.
My spirits were still low but Jether and Rafal both kept a steady eye on
me. Their concern was both touching and irritating. All that I desired
was to be left alone but they assured me by their actions that were the
last thing they would do. It did not help that our rations had been

nearly depleted. When Gideon made his rounds that night to check on everyone, he indicated that he was meeting with the town officials in the morning and would secure more provisions for us. Of course, that did not help us that evening. I obsessed over the wine and debated using hunger as an excuse to delve back into my stash. I didn't even have the energy to do that.

As we sat by the fire, the old man who had made the original journey with us came and sat by me at the fire. The frequency of his disappearances and reappearances baffled me but I figured it was none of my business, so I left the topic unbreached.

"How are you feeling, young man?"

I did not feel like a pep talk right now, so I decided a lie was easier. "Just enjoying the sunset." I had hoped my casual observation would be enough to put the old man off. Jether and Rafal had at least realized that talking to me was a wasted effort. They might not leave my side, but they did not barrage me with idle chatter.

"Sunsets can be a beautiful thing but a sunrise, a sunrise is something altogether different."

Was this man debating the merits of sunrises versus sunsets with me? I was not in the mood for small talk let alone an argument over nature's glory. "I don't like sunrises." This seemed to surprise the old man and he looked at me quizzically. If he had known how most of my days began, he would understand.

"Why is that?"

"I don't know. I have never liked sunrises. I feel like the sun is....judging me. It forces me awake to deal with all of the issues from the previous day when all I was trying to do was sleep."

"You are looking at it all wrong. The sunlight does not judge. It does not only shine on you and whatever problems you perceive to have. The sunrise projects light on everyone equally. It is filled with hope and opportunity, not judgment. Forgive me for saying so, but it seems like you see endings where He sees beginnings." With the word 'He', the old man pointed his finger upwards toward the sky. "Beginnings are wonderful things. They don't take the past into account. They just beckon you forward to start a new journey."

The old man put his hand on my shoulder and looked into the fire. "I hope that tomorrow's sunrise fills you with hope for a new beginning." He rose slowly, his arthritic knees cracking as he did so. I sat there, staring into the fire as well. I was not in the mood for an epiphany or revelation, so I just spread my blanket out and closed my eyes. My stomach ached from hunger but the words from the old man occupied my thoughts.

Of course, he was right. I did have a chance to start anew tomorrow. Would I still feel the same when the light from the sun found my eyes?

Chapter 23

The first thought that entered my mind the next morning was the sound of the birds nearby. Their song was a pleasant wake-up call to a new day. It took a monumental effort, but I tried to take the old man's words to heart. Today was a beginning. It was not an end. I opened my eyes and it was still dark out. I had gone to bed earlier than anyone else and I woke before anyone else. With all the stealth I could muster I reached for my sack with the other jug of wine. I was amazed that Rafal or Jether had not emptied it, but it was still heavy and full.

I removed the jug from the sack and quietly slipped away from the group. I found a space beyond the hill where we camped where no one could find me. I opened the jug and fell to my knees. I smelled the sweet scent and tears sprung to my eyes.

I whispered into the darkness with a ferocity that was not known to me before, "Dear Lord! Please remove this obsession from within me! Others live lives of beginnings and sunrises. Others laugh and enjoy each other's company. I want this. I want to be happy. I want my own beginning!" I slowly poured the wine onto the ground where it mixed with my falling tears. It was almost halfway gone and I had to desperately fight the urge not to turn it upwards and steal just a small drink. That would not do, though. If I was going to see a sunrise, it was going to be sober. My beginning would be fresh and pure. I kept pouring until it was gone and I dropped the jug on the ground and wept. My body shook with such force, I almost vomited on the spot. After indulging in this shameless lapse of control, I started to breathe slowly and deeply. My mind cycled between the regret of the wasteful action and optimism that drinking was no longer an option.

I knew there was no way for a new beginning if I had kept this crutch. I stood and looked over the horizon. At that moment, the first rays of sunlight for the day began to radiate from beyond the hills. I just stood and took the moment in. A fresh, cool breeze gave me chills up and down my body. I could do this. Whatever lay ahead, I would put my faith in God and accomplish what was called to be done.

I walked back to the camp where Rafal had sat up and was obviously waiting for me anxiously. He had noticed that the jug was gone, but with my steady gait and clear eyes, he knew that I had not drunk the wine. He smiled the most sincere smile I had ever seen.

"You were enjoying the sunrise?" He asked me hopefully.

"I was." I said, patting his back. I sat near the fire and started to arrange what little wood we had left to try and reignite the flames. We spent the morning finishing off the last of the rations we had. There was not much at all, but it was enough to last until fresh new bread was brought by the officials of Succoth. Around midday, Several men approached Gideon as he was talking to his men.

Gideon met the men and greeted them with his usual zealousness. **"Please give loaves of bread to the people who follow me, for they are exhausted, and I am pursuing after Zebah and Zalmunna, the kings of Midian."**

The leader of the group from Succoth reacted as if he had been slapped by Gideon himself. **""Are the hands of Zebah and Zalmunna already in your hand, that we should give bread to your army?"** It was Gideon's turn to take offense. Jether immediately lurched forward in defense of his father, but Gideon put an arm out to hold him back. He was tamed with one menacing glance from his father.

"Well then, when the LORD has given Zebah and Zalmunna into my hand, I will flail your flesh with the thorns of the wilderness and with briers."

The officials looked at one another and began to laugh. "You come here begging for food and then offer us threats in return. I should think not. You run along and fight your little battles but you will receive nothing from us!" The men turned to walk away and Gideon turned to face us.

I had yet to see such fury from Gideon and even I was frightened by his demeanor. I soon forgot about my hunger, I just wanted Gideon back to the way he was. He took a deep breath to collect himself. He looked out over the men and his eyes settled on mine. At least, I think they did. I guess that is what a leader does, makes everyone think they are talking to each and every person in the crowd.

"The time has come. You have shown how brave you are by simply being here. Now we must test the limits of that bravado. We fight. We end this now!" The men cheered. I was in no way compelled to scream at this proposition, so I just nodded. He had no idea how correct he was. My bravery would be put to the test and it terrified me on a profound level.

* * * * *

I stared at my feet as we stood near the top of the hill overlooking Karkor. We knew that Zebah and Zalmunna, the two kings of the eastern people had gathered the remaining 15,000 soldiers here. I stared at my feet, nearly covered by the ankle-high grass that had been dried by the afternoon sun. The breeze carried the noises that an army makes as it prepares for battle. There were shouts, the clanging of swords, and the braying of horses. They floated over the hill, whispering to us how outnumbered we still were.

I couldn't comprehend how they had lost over 100,000 soldiers since the campaign had begun, yet still outnumbered us fifty to one. I dwelled in the firmly held belief that I could not take a man's life, let alone fifty lives. I wiped the sweat from my forehead, dried my hand by running it through my hair, and grabbed the hilt of my knife. There were to be no tricks this time. Gideon had declared his intention. We were not to sneak up on them in the middle of the night and cause a chaotic scene like before. He said that God's glory would be displayed in the light of day this time.

I desperately wanted him to assuage my fears by telling us that God had promised each and every one of us would survive what was about to unfold, but he offered no such oaths. My heart beat faster than it had ever beaten before and I raised my eyes to look to my left. Rafal stood beside me, eyes closed in prayer, down on one knee. Jether was to my right and he looked more nervous than I had ever seen him before. This was the man who had sworn the army would shake in their armor at the mere sight of him. His body language displayed none of that confidence anymore.

I suddenly wished that Tabor and Amos were standing here with me again. The last time we had marched into what we believed would be a battle, I had the wine flowing in my veins to give me courage. There was no such luck this time.

This is not an ending.

This was a beginning.

I just kept repeating the mantra in my head over and over. The beginning of what? Life without any arms? Life with severe scars all over my body from the iron swords of the enemy? I took a deep breath and resigned to the fact that I very well could die this day. If that were the case, at least I would not be drunk, lying in a ditch somewhere, an embarrassment to what distant family I had left. No. If I died today, it would be in a glorious battle that history would remember forever, sober.

That is how my mind worked for the hour that we stood there. I cycled between moments of pure panic and moments of acceptance; almost a willingness to die. I still longed to hear God's voice for myself, but it was not to be.

"Men. Venture forth with me and honor our Father with bravery and skill." It was Gideon's voice, not God's. The words he spoke were filled with conviction, though and it steadied me a bit. He slowly treads up to the top of the hill and looked down. I did not want to witness what he was seeing, but everyone else stepped forward as well. The effort that it took to take the first step was more than any I can ever remember. I took a few more steps and it got a little easier with each one. By the time I reached the crest of the ridge, I felt that my heart would suddenly explode. I looked down at the army we would be engaging with only moments from now and an audible gasp escaped my lips. By now, I had seen bigger armies, but 15,000 men are 15,000 men. The enormity of the situation was cemented in my brain and I wished for nothing more than to turn and run. Dying, drunk in a ditch, didn't seem so bad compared to the marauders we would be running towards.

"A sword for the Lord and for Gideon!" He yelled, just as he had before. This time, I was not inspired. He immediately began to sprint down the hill. I instinctively followed. I can only imagine how pathetic our pack of three hundred men looked descending upon them. I tried to push this thought aside and began to pray as I'd never prayed before.

Lord, please keep me safe. I am trying to honor You, please reward me with victory in Your name!

It felt like it took us half the day to reach their front lines, but it couldn't have been more than a few moments. I watched Gideon raise his mighty sword and deliver a blow that glanced off the helmet of what I assumed was a Midianite. The sword removed the man's ear and shot blood from the side of his head. The man's hand immediately released the hilt of his sword and was raised to the side of his head where blood continued to pour from between his fingers. It was then that Gideon impaled him with his sword and kicked him off. He fell to the ground, dying slowly, moans emanating from the freshly dispatched mound of flesh covered in an armor that had failed him miserably.

I was viciously ripped from being a spectator to an unwilling participant when I felt a foot on my chest. I tumbled backward and lay prone on the ground until I remembered I had a knife in my right hand. I raised it and the man who had kicked me found the blade of my weapon with his neck as he attempted to engage me in battle. My first kill and I had participated as minimally as possible. On my back with this man on top of me, I could feel his warm blood on my hand. My shocked paralysis ended with a horrific realization that the gurgling victim was dying on top of me. I shoved him off and tried to stand. I stumbled backward as if I had finished the wine instead of pouring it on the ground. I stared at the man when I heard someone yell from somewhere beside me.

"Look out! Keep fighting!" It sounded like Rafal but I had no time to investigate as I saw a man with an ax quickly approaching me. Again, I failed to remember that I had a knife and simply grabbed the arm that held the ax. The man grunted and shoved me aside. As he did so, he ambled forward, exposing his back to me and I quickly plunged my knife into his side. He fell to his knees and swung his ax backward. The wild swipe missed me and I stabbed him again, slightly higher in his side. He dropped the ax and clutched his ribs in agony. I stepped forward, further into battle. I had no time to wait and see if he was, in fact, dead. There were impending targets still approaching.

In the corner of my eye, I saw Gideon sprinting through the army like a man possessed by spirits. What was his destination, the rear of the column?

Another man approached, this time the figure in front of me wielded a sword that was obviously too heavy for him to use efficiently. The time that it took for him to raise it, gave me ample opportunity to sink my knife into the soft spot below his chin. He died almost immediately. The force of my removing the knife from his body sent me backward and I fell once more. I was face to face with the man who had previously held the ax. He was still alive and clutching his side.

"I'm so sorry." I inexplicably said to the man I had attempted to murder. I had no idea where the words came from but I could think of nothing else to say. In my mind, he was most likely an unwilling participant in this grand game of checkers that kings played with real men. I forced myself up again and noticed that Rafal had also fallen. He had a man on top of him and was losing his test of strength with a man that held a mace. Since he was not looking at me, it made it easy for me to dispatch my fourth victim. While he slowly subdued Rafal, I sank my knife deeply into the man's temple. Only forty-six more to go. Rafal looked at me with gratitude and nodded. No words were exchanged but he jumped up with a grace I would have never been able to display.

It had only been a few minutes of physical activity but my muscles burned like never before. It was at this point when I doubted my physical ability to continue, then something took over me. I can't say for sure that my prayers had been answered but I began to move with a speed and grace that I had previously not possessed. I swung my knife left and right and was able to push the repercussions of my actions to the back of my mind. I made my way further and further into the crowd as the bodies of my victims lay at my feet.

There was a brief moment when there was no one to engage in battle with and I took the opportunity to wipe the blood and sweat from my face. Rafal and Jether were hacking their way forward as well, with no physical evidence of sustaining any wounds. The battle was going well and I felt hope spring deep within me. It was the first time that I harbored hope of surviving this ordeal.

Then a shadow fell over me. The largest man I had ever seen stood before me. He had murder in his eyes. In fact, his eyes were all that I could see because the rest of him was covered with leather armor. He swung an ax horizontally, aimed at my head. I dropped to my knees and stabbed my knife forward into his thigh. It pierced the leather and I could not retract it. The direct hit had no impact on the veracity of my attacker and he simply kicked me away. He brought the ax above his head and brought it down with all of his might. I rolled to my side, exposing my back to him. He brought his foot down midroll, pinning me to the ground.

I could see Jether to my left, still fighting. There would be no one to save me from certain death this time. I used my arms to push up as violently as I could and this seemed to knock the man off balance. I whipped around and drove my shoulder into his stomach. He let out a large grunt and we both tumbled into a pile of bodies. I put both of my hands on the side of his head and jerked his helmet off. I heard a snap and he let out a guttural scream. He then wrapped his arms around me and started squeezing.

The air slowly left my body and I could start to see stars dancing in front of me. My attacker had no intention of letting go and he somehow found the energy to squeeze harder and harder. I thrust the top of my head into his face and he screamed in pain again, or was it me? It had the same effect on me as razor-sharp burns streaked down my head. I forced myself to do it over and over again until I felt his arms loosen around me. I brought my knee up sharply and made contact between his legs.

He let go and rolled over. I fell off of him and did the same. Moments passed and then I felt his fist land square into my lower back. I was dizzy and nauseous and got up on one knee. I looked toward him but only saw a blurry figure that vaguely resembled the man who had nearly constricted the life out of me. He stood up again and stumbled backward and forward once more. I lunged for the knife that was still stuck in the armor covering his thigh. I placed my foot on his stomach and yanked as hard as I could until it became free.

He reached down and grabbed his ax, showing his bare neck to me, and with a lightning-quick reflex, I plunged my knife deep into his neck. My vision was completely obscured by the copious amounts of blood that spurted from the wound. He fell to the ground and I, was on top of him.

I had done it. I had defeated him. I hoped it would be the last man that I would ever have to kill. It was at that moment that the battle turned even more chaotic. There was a panic that could be felt rising up among the Midianites. They began to scramble and evacuate the battlefield as if they were on fire. Even if I wanted to continue fighting, there was no one remotely near me to do so with. I looked up into the horizon hoping to catch a glimpse of what had caused the mass scattering of Midianites and I saw Gideon chasing two figures far away from the battlefield. All three were on horses and looked to be fleeing the battleground.

"He is going after the kings!" Rafal shouted. "They are retreating, the Midianites are as well!" He stood over a man who was writhing in his death throes and a big grin spread across his face.

"That was all it took?" I uttered, not loud enough to be heard. Gideon must have known that without the head of the snake, it would wither and die. I felt an arm around my shoulders and whipped towards the source, prepared to skewer another man. Jether stepped back in shock.

"Whoa there, mighty warrior. It is just me. A fellow conqueror." Jether said with a confident air about him.

"We have done it?" I questioned, still not able to believe that it was over.

"I imagine we have." Jether said as we watched the backs of the few Midianites that survived scatter off into the distance.

"We...we have won?"

Rafal laughed, "Do not look so surprised, Ethan. The victory was promised to us long ago. This is the day that was inevitable. We are free from those heathens. God has delivered us what was guaranteed."

I dropped to my knees immediately. My body, riding so high on the physical fight, now fell apart. Every muscle that I could identify ached to some degree. My vision was still blurred and my head throbbed. I wept. My body shook and all the emotions poured out of me unabashedly.

Chapter 24

Gideon had not returned but there was no apprehension at his absence. We found a place on the battlefield, far away from the dead, and basked in the sun.

"Do you know if any of us did not make it?" I asked my two new friends. I didn't expect an answer since they had been fighting by my side and probably had as much knowledge of the situation as I did.

Jether popped up to his feet. "I do not, but I intend to find out." With that declaration, he leaped into action. He began counting our meager numbers. Within the hour he had returned.

"Three hundred men, all stand victorious and well." He could not wipe the grin off his face and sat back down. I marveled at the energy the young man still employed after such a vigorous exercise. The images of the men that I had killed would sneak into the forefront of my mind but I was able to push them away. I imagined I would have plenty of time to relive those horrors in my dreams, there was no sense in indulging in the practice while still awake.

"I am sure your father is alive and well too, Jether." I offered to try and comfort him.

"There is not a doubt in my mind. I am sure that he will return with the head of both kings shortly and this will all officially be over."

He sounded confident in the assertion and it proved to be true the next day. Mid-morning, Gideon approached the camp with the two kings, though their bodies were still attached. They had been tied up with rope and walked behind his horse. Their faces were dirty but otherwise unharmed.

"Men!" Gideon shouted when he was within earshot. "You are victorious!" We all cheered with a renewed spirit. "You answered God's call and you are now witnessing to the greatest military victory in history. Your names will be remembered for generations to come!"

I was relatively sure that only Gideon's name would be memorialized in this campaign, but I was willing to play along for now. He dismounted his horse and brought the two kings before us.

"I have promised their heads and I will deliver. Men, our mission is almost completed. We are to return to Succoth and fulfill our oath to the elders. Ride with me once more will you?" There were cheers, though less hardy this time, and we each rose to our feet and headed for our camels.

On our trek, we encountered a young man who claimed to be from Succoth and Gideon requested that he write down the names of the seventy-seven elders from the village. We were ordered to collect thorns from the wilderness and briers as we rode. I was stunned that he had every intention of beating the elders as he had promised prior to the battle. This should not have surprised me. Gideon had proven time and time again to be a man of his word. Upon our arrival, he called them before us and took attendance. All of them were there.

"Behold Zebah and Zalmunna, about whom you taunted me, saying, 'Are the hands of Zebah and Zalmunna already in your hand, that we should give bread to your men who are exhausted?' Gideon called to them, his voice echoing majestically through the surrounding hills. None of the officials answered this question and Gideon stepped down from his horse once more. He took the thorns and briers and whipped them until they were bloodied, one by one.

I have to say, it was the most awkward, yet satisfying, display of revenge that I had ever witnessed and it seemed to take forever. Some of our three hundred soldiers laughed at the display but I found no humor in it. I just happened to be blessed to be on the right side of this whole ordeal. I did not claim to know the hearts of these men but I knew in my heart, I would be happy to never witness another violent act as long as I lived.

After that, we were ordered to destroy a tower that they had built to honor another God. Many of the men cried and their fear was evident on their faces. I held one of the ropes that tore down the tower and pictured the temple of Ba'al at Rimmon where I had spent so much of my time. I felt hypocritical but also realized that I had become a different man now.

I was also thankful that I was involved in the destruction of the tower because the other assignment was to kill the rest of the men in the city and I wanted no part of that. A message was definitely being sent. The Israelites would no longer be slaves. We were to be free and unmolested by any outsiders near our lands. For that, I was thankful.

The night was beginning to fall in Succoth and when the destruction was over, we reconvened just outside of the village. The two kings sat, humiliated and defeated at the hooves of our camels. Gideon approached Zebah and Zalmunna.

"Where are the men whom you killed at Tabor?" They answered, "As you are, so were they. Every one of them resembled the son of a king." And he said, "They were my brothers, the sons of my mother. As the LORD lives, if you had saved them alive, I would not kill you."

Gideon turned to Jether and said, **"Rise and kill them!"**

We looked at Jether and he was suddenly a shell of the boisterous warrior he was the day before. He was visibly shaken by this order and he displayed an unwillingness to kill the royalty that stood before him. I'm not sure if it was because they were kings or he had just tired of killing, but it was obvious that he had no intention of carrying this order out.

"I do not wish to behead these men, father." He said sheepishly.

Gideon looked disappointed but he did not want to quarrel with his son in front of all of the men.

"Rise yourself and fall upon us, for as the man is, so is his strength." Zebah responded.

The men simultaneously turned their heads to look at the king who had ordered his own death. Gideon turned, with malice in his eyes, towards the source of the challenge. In one swift motion, he drew his sword, cocked his arm back, and impaled the former king. He repeated the action for Zalmunna, bringing an end to our war. I averted my eyes for the second execution, again longing to return home and begin my life of peace.

Gideon took the heads of the kings and adorned his camels with them. Gideon was definitely a different breed. I was content with my camel just as it was. The next day we began our march back to where we started. We encountered throngs of elated Israelites along the way who begged Gideon to become king. Each and every offer was rejected by Gideon, showing his humility before God. I had grown to love this man.

Chapter 25

The sun had nearly fallen from the sky and a breeze filled the valley. The calls of birds in the distance filled the bittersweet air. It was time for our farewell. Gideon stood squarely in the middle of the intersection of several paths that would lead to our separate departures. Tears gently rested in his eyes as he scanned each and every one of us. He tried and stuttered through a couple of attempts, but a lump prevented his usual demonstrative speech. After taking a few minutes to compose himself, he began once more.

"Brothers! It has been an honor to live, fight, cry, laugh, and worship with each and every man here. What we have done, has brought truly wondrous glory to God. Our names will forever be synonymous with faith and duty. What greater legacy could we possibly hope to leave behind?

Each of you has grown so much in character since our campaign began. I pray that you take what you have seen and continue to learn and feel the love and favor of our Creator. Some of you will return to families, others will travel home in solitude. Regardless of where your home is and who resides in it, know that you have three hundred brothers scattered throughout the land who will forever be by your side when you need it the most.

We may be saying goodbye, but that is not the end of the story. This has been but a chapter in what will surely be an inspiring tale that you are the sole author of. Say your goodbyes to each other, but never abandon the relationships you have been blessed with. The fights we fought were truly epic in scope, but it was the little moments we spent by the campfires that you will treasure forever. The moments of laughter while walking through the wilderness you should hold close to your heart. I hope the tears that were shed by brothers who missed their loved ones will forever remind you how much God has given us. May we never take any of these memories for granted.

We came together to honor God and that is what we did. I pray that you do not stop trying to honor Him each and every day of the rest of your lives. Thank you for your service and go in peace, brothers. I love each and every one of you."

Tears streamed down Gideon's face as Jether embraced his father. I turned to Rafal and embraced him as well.

"I have never thanked you for saving my life on the field of battle that day, my friend." Rafal whispered into my ear. We broke our embrace and stared into his eyes.

"It was you who saved my life, Rafal. I will be forever grateful for each and every experience that we shared. You pulled me from a tomb and gave me new life. How does one repay such a debt?" I replied.

"By doing what Gideon said. Remembering that we are brothers and honoring God to the best of your abilities for all the days of your life remaining. What are your plans now? It breaks my heart to think of you returning to your homeland alone."

I thought for a few moments. I had no plan. I had ideas and options, but no plans. "I will not be alone. Hopefully, Tabor and Amos will still be there. I will rebuild and start again, I guess."

Rafal nodded, obviously not satisfied with the plan. It was probably the lack of conviction in my voice when I said this. "I hear Golan is beautiful this time of year. Rolling hills and beautiful vistas as far as the eye can see." Rafal smiled as he nudged my shoulder.

I furrowed my brow a bit and said, "You know, that does sound like a good idea. I will return home and settle my affairs, but I think I may just take you up on the offer."

"That is good to hear. I will tell Yaffa...I mean, my family that you are coming. The offer is always open. Take as long as you need. As Gideon said, we are life-long brothers. My door will always be open to you."

"And mine as well. I mean, as soon as I get a door."

Rafal laughed, "Farewell, Ethan. I will see you soon."

"Farewell and peace be with you Rafal."

Rafal widened his eyes in surprise. "A righteous man he is now! Peace be with you and I pray for your safe journey."

I started to walk away and looked for Gideon. I'm sure that he was surrounded by men clamoring to bend his ear one last time. I was just starting to feel the disappointment at having to leave his company when he appeared in front of me with Jether by his side.

"Ethan! You were not going to leave without saying goodbye, were you?" Gideon said, taking mock offense at the idea.

"That was not my intention, but I assumed you were occupied by others."

"From this day forward, brother, I will always be available to you. You know where to find me. I am returning home to Ophrah. I hope to increase the size of my family a great deal and live out my life in peace!"

I smiled, "Maybe have a child who listens to you a little better than this one." I said motioning towards Jether. I cringed as soon as I spoke the words, not knowing if it was a sore spot between the two but both of them laughed heartily.

"One of them will be bound to." Gideon responded as he wrapped his arm around his son.

"Gideon, I just wanted to say..." I froze. I could not find the words profound enough to illustrate my admiration and sincerity. "Thank you...for...for everything." I stammered in frustration.

"There is no need for poetry, Ethan. There is no perfect phrase or combination of words necessary between families. You may think you owe me something but you do not. It was just as much an honor for me to serve by your side. It was truly an inspiration to see how much you changed and all the glory goes to God. You leave here a different man than the one that arrived and it has been a pleasure to witness. You may not see it in yourself, but you truly are a leader of men."

The image of me, bloodied in a cave, moments from taking my own life, craving a sip of wine flashed through my mind. I was not that man anymore.

"There will be a part of you in everything I do from this day forward. I pray that our paths cross again one day." I said.

"Yes! Pray. Pray as much as you can. That is the only true way to make it through this life we live. Peace be with you, Ethan." He embraced me and a tear slipped from my eye. I whispered 'and peace be with you, Gideon in his ear. I repeated the same thing to Jether as we embraced and then watched them walk away.

He would say personalized goodbyes to each and every man that day and into the night as we all departed down different paths. Men stood in line for the chance to say goodbye to him. He wouldn't have had it any other way. That was just his nature, his character.

As I started down the path on my very own camel, with my grain bags filled with loot to help me get started again, I pondered how my worldview had changed in such a short time. I had gone from a man of distracted faith to one of focus and purpose. I had witnessed how God can use anyone or anything to show his glory, power, and love. The overwhelming realization that God had chosen to use me as his tool hit me in waves during my trek home. I camped where I could, prayed often, and pondered what the next chapter of my life would look like.

For the first time in my life, anything seemed possible.

Chapter 26

I stood at the crest of the hill that overlooked Rimmon, the sun setting to my left.. I had missed this geographical location more than I realized. I took a deep breath and started to descend the hill. I had purposely approached from the south to avoid going through the main streets. I had long envisioned returning the conquering hero, but I felt I needed a moment before seeing Tabor, Amos, the wine shop, the temple of Ba'al, or anyone for that matter. I would return to my pile of rubble and sleep for the night and visit with my friends in the morning when I was well rested.

I neared my land, taking in every familiar landmark with a newfound appreciation for each and every detail. It was unusually noisy with the clattering of construction as I breached the tree line bordering my property. My breath left my body. On my land, twenty people were nearing the end of a construction project. The structure of a house three times the size of my previous domicile was nearly completed. Someone had stripped me of my property and had the audacity to build a house on the site of my childhood home.

Fury welled inside of me as my heart beat faster and my face burned with anger. I started to walk briskly toward the thieving group of bandits.

"What are you doing on my land!" I screamed when I was close enough to be heard.

Some of the men who were placing bricks on top of each other looked around at the boisterous intruder. At that moment, Tabor and Amos both exited the door with broad smiles on their faces.

Tabor was the first to speak, "The conquering hero returns home too early for his own good! Gentlemen, welcome the king home to his new throne room!" Tabor said, waving his arm grandly at the incomplete structure. I froze in my tracks.

"This...this is for me?" I muttered, once again lost for words.

"Unless you have sold the property to someone else." Amos said.

"No. Why? How did you...?"

Tabor embraced me and stepped back and said, "There was no way that we were going to let you come back to a pile of bricks after what you have accomplished. Once the Midianites proved to be no match for your mighty army, we got a few men together and decided to build you a proper home. Do you like it?"

"Of course! It is glorious." I could barely speak. More tears came to my eyes and I wondered how many more I had left. I tried to cover up my emotional instability by quipping, "I'm not a big fan of that big hole in the side, though. Can you patch that up?"

Tabor laughed, "We aren't finished yet, you imbecile. Finally, you can start pitching in and giving us a hand, you lazy, no-good-for-nothing ingrate. But first, tell us everything!"

I walked over to my new home where strangers I had never met greeted me with congratulations and thank-yous. I recognized some faces from around town, but to my shame, I had never made the attempt to get to know them. A fire was burning near the construction site and a few of the men sat with Tabor, Amos, and me.

"I can't thank you enough for this. It was the last thing I expected to see upon my return." I started as the food was passed around the fire. I immediately shoved the food in my mouth to quell the ravishing hunger inside of me. When I finished swallowing, I added, "I thought you would be upset with me for staying."

Amos responded, "We were more than a little upset at first, but it was never at you. We were more disturbed with Gideon."

"After a while, the feeling of being rejected died down a little and we figured we might as well do something productive. With the Midianites out of the area, we figured it would be safe to start rebuilding." Tabor said.

We stayed up into the early hours of the morning. I told them about Rafal and Jether. I recounted our first battle and their jaws dropped. They were riveted by my tales of fighting glory and by the end of the story, I could tell they had a better understanding of Gideon's reasons why a commander of an army would dismiss most of his army on the eve of battle. It was one of the best nights of my life and I never once thought of wine.

* * * * *

A few days later, my new home was finished. I stood with Amos and Tabor outside the walls of the freshly constructed structure with more gratitude in my heart than I could ever express.

"It's a good house to raise a family in." Amos said with a sideways glance.

I nodded. "I have been meaning to broach that topic with you guys." I said sheepishly.

They both looked over at me with surprised looks. "Go on." Tabor encouraged.

"I may have just the idea of how to complete that goal. It involves a trip to Golan."

"What is in Golan?" Amos asked.

"I'm not sure yet. It may amount to nothing, but I feel like I owe it to myself to find out. Remember Rafal, the man who befriended me once you guys abandoned me? He has a sister that he wants me to meet. I believe I am going to take him up on the invitation."

Tabor patted me on the back enthusiastically, "Look at you! Ethan, world traveler. Hadn't left Rimmon his entire life and now you are practically an explorer. Is this sister particularly attractive?" Tabor asked with a mischievous grin.

I looked at him with mock disgust, "I am not concerned with such things. Anyway, I'm going to go and just meet her. No promises or oaths have been made. Nothing may come of it, but as I said, I owe it to myself. One can't just piddle his life away on a farm in isolation."

"So I guess you expect us to take care of your farm while you are off wife-hunting?" Amos said.

"What farm? It's just dirt!" I said.

"Who is going to feed all of your sheep and harvest all the wheat that has been donated to you by the people of Rimmon?" Tabor asked with a guileless smile.

I whipped my head around. "Are you serious?"

Amos nodded, "The sheep have already been pledged, they were just waiting on your return. The wheat has been planted. It is the debt that the people owe you. We are no longer imprisoned, destined for poverty. That is because of you. The people know it and are happy to help."

I was astonished beyond belief. God was good. I had not even prayed for such generosity and yet he poured his mercy out on me nonetheless. I looked around my property and at my friends, a smile cemented my face. I had everything I needed. I had gone to war with nothing and returned with everything. I had won my war.

Chapter 27

I woke up, yet didn't open my eyes. I just lay in the dark and thought about what the day held for me. It reminded me of forty years earlier. Those cursed days of waking up in fear of the sun's judgment, trying to figure out what I had done the night before. Those days are long gone now. I hadn't had a drop of wine to drink in forty years. The only difficulty in waking up now was the aches in pains that emanated from my aging body.

I said my morning prayer, as I always did now. I thanked him for Yaffa who lay quietly snoring beside me. I gave thanks for the ability to make this journey that we were on and I prayed for the strength to make it through this solemn day. If it was to be done, it might as well be done now.

I pushed myself up and stretched. My legs cracked and popped loud enough to wake Yaffa up. We had left the kids behind so that we could spend a little time alone. I did not tell her that I was afraid of my emotional state and did not want the children to see their father in shambles. They did not mind staying back in Rimmon. After all, they were inseparable from their friends, Tabor and Amos' children.

"Are you well?" Yaffa asked as she put her hand on my back.

"I am just thankful that you are here with me." I leaned down and gave her a kiss.

"Of course. I would hate to think of you making this trip alone."

We dressed in the comfortable silence of a man and woman who had spent most of their lives together. It truly was a blessing to have her near me. This was going to be more difficult than anything I could remember. I stood at the door of the inn, dreading what was to come. Yaffa squeezed my hand and we opened it to start the day.

We stepped into the busy streets and blended in with the men and women going about their business. My body tensed when we passed through the center of town. Tall stone pillars were being erected at the future site of the newest temple to Ba'al in the region.

"I fear that we will never learn." I said to Yaffa.

She shook her head in disgust. "I guess it was inevitable. All we can do is stay vigilant in prayer and have faith. You of all people know what God can do."

"I do and that is why it scares me sometimes. Of course, you are right though. The tension in my body started to dissipate once we left the main thoroughfare. We headed towards the hills in the east. Our destination was a little uncertain but I found a reliable source in town to help me find what I was looking for.

We started to climb the hill where the brush had been freshly burned to make room for crops. We found an awkward grove of trees and then started to ascend a footpath up some rocky terrain. For the first time, I began to fear that my body was too old for this journey. Yaffa was breathing hard and I felt as if my knees were going to give out at any second. I prayed for strength for this one last obligation.

My fear of not being able to find my destination was unfounded for when we approached a sealed-off cave, dozens of flowers and monuments were laid on the stone of a large boulder.

This was it.

Yaffa and I exchanged glances and she knew to step back and give me some distance. Unspoken love and affection bolstered me in this tenuous moment. I slowly stepped forward and kneeled at the foot of the large rock that blocked the entrance to the cave. I put my hand on the boulder, closed my eyes, and bowed my head.

"Hello, old friend." and the tears started again. "The deepest regret that I have is that I never came to visit you before now. For that, I apologize sincerely. After everything that you meant to me, I should have made the effort.

I just wanted to say thank you one last time. My life started on the day that I met you. Before that moment, I was nothing but a hopeless drunk with no direction in life. You chose to not see that in me. When someone willfully decides to see what you could be instead of what you are, it changes a man. Because of you, I was able to stop drinking, find a wife, and have eleven children. Of course, that was nothing compared to how many you had! I am happy. I have a home and land that I raise sheep on. I have never known hunger since that day at Succoth.

I have lived in peace for the last forty years of my life. I pray often, all day every day. You were right. There is no other way to make it through life in one piece than to live in constant communication with our heavenly father. My children are righteous and pray often as well. My beautiful, loving wife has raised them well.

All of this is because I happened to drunkenly stumble into your path. Gideon, I miss you. I wish you could have met my family. All of Israel owes you so much. I do not grieve your death, because I know that you will spend eternity with the Almighty, I only grieve that I never get to see your face again or hear that enthusiastic voice again. You had the ability to make everyone their best. When you talked to people, you made them feel as if they were the only ones around. It is a unique skill that I have tried my best to replicate. This world so desperately needs more of that.

The passion, grace, and bravery that you lived with was an inspiration to all."

I stopped and broke down sobbing. Yaffa was quickly at my side with her hand on my shoulder. She reached up with her other hand and softly touched the rock.

"I wish you could have met him." I choked through my sobs.

"I do as well. Rafal had nothing but great things to say about him. He talked about him often."

"It was all true." I said.

I turned my attention back to Gideon's tomb. "I'm going to go now, old friend. I hope you rest in peace and watch over us. I fear for the future. I fear the people of Israel will once again turn their backs on

God. But one thing I do not fear for is my soul. As far as that battle is concerned, I already know who won."